Annalisa's
JOURNEY THROUGH
Grief

JUDITH
AND
PAUL VANDER WEGE

Printed in the United States of America

ISBN 979-8-89114-036-3 (sc)
ISBN 979-8-89114-037-0 (e)

Library of Congress Control Number: 2023923283

2024.01.18

MainSpring Books
5901 W. Century Blvd
Suite 750
Los Angeles, CA, US, 90045

www.mainspringbooks.com

Dedicated to those hurting from the grief of lost loved ones and/or the injustice of bullying. May you know God loves you and will strengthen you for your journey, if you ask Him.

Contents

1

Annalisa's Shocking News

S trains of Pachelbel's Canon filled the air. When her phone interrupted the peaceful music, Annalisa's heart jumped. She snatched the smart phone out of her pocket. Seeing that it was her best friend, she sighed with relief. "Hi, Mary Lou. What are you up to?"

"Hi Annalisa. Know what? There's a sale at the mall. Wanna go look for those shoes?"

"Yes, I'd like that. It'll be fun to spend some time with you...take my mind off being so anxious for my parents to come home from the mission trip."

"When are they supposed to come?"

"Any day now."

"Let's meet at 1:00 by the shoe store."

"Right. See you then."

"Oh, by the way Annalisa, I've been meaning to tell you how sorry I am about what happened between you and Brenda yesterday."

"Thanks. She sure seemed upset..."

"Well, she didn't need to take it out on you! How dare she push you down and call you Smarty Pants!"

"Oh, I don't think she pushed me down on purpose. We just ran into each other."

"It looked to me like she ran into you on purpose. Did you see how mad she looked? Then she didn't even help you pick up your books and papers that scattered all over."

"It did hurt. I wonder what was bothering her." Annalisa rubbed her sore elbow.

"None of the girls like her," Mary Lou continued. "She's so mean and stuck up."

"That's too bad. I wonder why she acts like that."

Mary Lou cleared her throat. "I don't know and I don't care. I just don't want her hurting my best friend who's always so sweet."

"Thanks, Mary Lou. I'll see you at 1:00."

Annalisa stood up and put her phone back in her pocket. As she headed toward the kitchen for lunch, Annalisa glanced out the front window. What a beautiful day for an outing at the mall with her best friend. She and her aunt, who was staying with her for the two weeks her parents were gone, chatted pleasantly as they ate.

Several minutes later, she glanced out the window again. "Oh no!" Annalisa exclaimed. Dread gripped her mind as she saw her pastor coming up the walk. She jumped up from the lunch table and ran to open the door. Staring at the somber man, she asked, "Has something happened to Mom and Dad?"

Her aunt rushed to her side. "Annalisa, what's wrong? Oh--- hello, Pastor Brady." Catherine looked puzzled. "What's wrong?"

"Hello Annalisa, Catherine. Please, may I come in? Could we go sit down?"

After they were seated in the living room, Pastor Brady cleared his throat. "I'm sorry—I have come with terrible news." He paused, apparently fighting to stay calm. "There was an airplane accident on their way home…"

Annalisa gasped. "Dad and Mom crashed?" she asked, incredulous. "Are they … dead?"

Pastor Brady coughed, then spoke in a strangled voice, "Yes, as well as the entire group."

Annalisa felt like a hammer hit her chest and took her voice away, then she began sinking into a deep hole. *This can't be true. How could God not have protected them while they were on a mission trip for him?* She felt Catherine sit down beside her on the love seat, trembling.

Pastor looked at them intently from the closest chair. He explained in a strained voice, "The plane in which they flew developed engine trouble, lost two engines, and crashed into a mountain side after takeoff. Those who found it said everyone on board died."

Annalisa moaned, then blurted out, "I told them not to go!" she hit her fist on the arm of the love seat. "Ecuador is too dangerous. I knew something terrible would happen!"

Now that she knew her worst fears had been realized, she began sobbing hysterically. Aunt Catherine reached over and held her tight, her own sobs blending in and tears falling on Annalisa's hair.

After a few minutes, Pastor Brady rose and put a hand gently on each one's shoulder. "I'm so sorry to have to bring you such sad news. I'll stay with you for awhile." His voice sounded husky. He wiped his eyes, sat down and blew his nose.

"Oh, God no-o-o! Why …?" Annalisa covered her face with her hands. *This must be a nightmare,* she thought.

Aunt Catherine continued to hold Annalisa as they both shook with sobs. Finally she assured Annalisa, "I love you, honey. I'll stay here with you." Her voice sounded strained as she said, "We'll make it through."

The Pastor sat with his hands folded and head bowed. When the sobbing had calmed down, he asked, "May we pray together?"

Annalisa nodded with downcast eyes. Catherine said, "Please do." Annalisa glanced at her and saw her eyes filled with anguish.

"Father in Heaven," prayed Pastor Brady, "We don't understand why this has happened, but we pray that you would help and comfort Annalisa, who has lost her beloved father and mother. Wrap your loving arms around her and give her peace of heart and mind, and strength for what she faces now and in the future. Help and comfort Catherine, too, who has lost her brother and sister-in-law. As she stays with Annalisa, help her to be a loving and helpful guide, now and in the future. Help me, as their Pastor to help them both, as well as the others who have lost loved ones. We thank you, Lord, that we know Marcia and Bob have committed their lives to you. Therefore we know we can see them again in Heaven. We pray this in Jesus' name, Amen."

Annalisa mopped at her eyes and blew her nose. She felt like her heart was breaking. How could she cope with not having her loving and wise mom and dad around? She felt so alone. After sitting quietly a few minutes, she looked up. She swallowed the lump in her throat, wiping her eyes again. "Thank you, Pastor and Aunt Catherine, for being with me."

Catherine squeezed her hand.

"You are welcome," said Pastor Brady. He reached out and touched her other hand. "I have to go talk to others now, but will come back after church and lunch tomorrow and help you with arrangements."

"You will have a lot of funerals to do, won't you?" Catherine asked him, quietly.

"Yes, or we might have a group service. I haven't talked to everyone yet." Pastor sighed.

Annalisa sighed, too, then lifted her chin. "I think a group service is a good idea." She looked first at Aunt Catherine, then the Pastor. "Maybe we can all comfort each other."

Pastor looked at Catherine, who nodded in agreement. "Thanks, that will help." He stood up. "Bye. See you tomorrow."

After the Pastor let himself out, Catherine and Annalisa continued sitting together, numb, for several moments. "I'm scared, Aunt Catherine," Annalisa whispered. "I feel so alone."

"I know. I'm scared, too," admitted her aunt, stroking her hair. "But you're not alone. I'll stay with you, as I said. Besides, we are not as those who have no hope, as it says in the Bible. The Holy Spirit of our Savior is our comforter and guide and will help us know what to do."

"Mom always said I needed to trust God." She clenched her fists. "But how can I trust God when he let this happen to people who were serving him? What's the point of that?" She stood up and began pacing, hitting one fist against her other palm. "I'm not sure I can do that!"

"This is a question many people down through the ages have asked. We may never know the answer. However, God is holy and righteous. Because Jesus died in our place and rose again, we can know God loves us and is able to use evil for good in our lives." Catherine stood up and hugged her niece again and nuzzled her face in her hair as she said, "I'm certain God loves us."

Annalisa leaned back and faced her aunt. "You were planning to stay only these two or three weeks. Don't you need to get back to work?"

"Helping you through this grief takes priority. It will help me with my grief, also. I'll tell my boss what happened and give him a letter of resignation. I didn't really like living in the city anyway. I can find a day job here and be home with you in the evenings."

"Thank you." Annalisa took her hand. Tears ran quietly down her cheeks.

"You are welcome, my dear." They both wiped their tears and sat down again.

Suddenly, the phone rang. "Oh, I suppose that's Mary Lou wondering where I am. I told her I'd meet her at the mall at 1 o'clock." Annalisa took her smart phone out of her pocket and explained to her friend, with tears running down her cheeks, what had happened. "Will you come over later? Thanks, that will help."

"Mary Lou will come this evening for a while," she told Catherine, putting the phone away. After several moments of silence, Annalisa asked. "Is there something we need to do before we talk to Pastor again tomorrow?"

"Do you know if your parents have a will?"

"Yes, just a few weeks ago they said they were going to update their will. They went to a lawyer, Mr. Nathan Page. I didn't pay much attention at the time because they assured me that making a will was just standard procedure, and they didn't expect to die soon."

"Since it's Saturday pm, I'm sure his office is closed. Do you want to try calling him at home to see if he can meet with us first thing Monday morning? Or would you like me to? Or we could just wait until Monday morning."

"I think I should tell him, at least," said Annalisa. "He was a friend with Mom and Dad as well as their lawyer. I'll call him." She found Nathan Page's home number, and dialed it. When he answered, she said, "This is Annalisa Schuiteman calling. I believe you recently helped my parents update their will?"

"Yes, I did."

"I just found out my parents died … in a plane crash..." (Annalisa choked up and couldn't speak for several seconds, but fought for control)... "in Ecuador." After forcing out those words, Annalisa broke down in sobs. She slunk to the floor, still holding the phone to her ear.

"Oh, Annalisa, That's terrible!" Nathan Page said. "I'm so sorry for you!"

When Annalisa could speak again, she asked, "Could my aunt and I meet with you Monday morning to talk about the will?"

"Did your parents tell you about it?"

"If they did, I don't remember. They acted like it was something I'd never need to see."

"If you'd like, I could come over now and show it to you. I know at a time like this it could be frightening and awfully hard to wait until Monday."

"Oh, that would be so kind of you! Yes, please do come." Annalisa hung up and looked at Catherine, who stood next to her with her mouth open.

"Did he say he's coming here? Now?" Catherine asked.

Annalisa nodded with a slight smile of relief.

"I've never heard of a lawyer making a house call."

"He goes to our church. He and his wife are, rather were, friends of Mom and Dad."

"Well, I think we might be able to sleep better if we know what's what, so I'm glad he's coming. I'll put the tea kettle on to heat. It may take him a while to explain it all to us."

"I'm glad he's coming, too." Annalisa said.

The lawyer arrived in about twenty minutes. "I had to go by the office to get the will, and then took time to make a copy you can keep." They all sat down at the dining room table after Annalisa introduced him to her aunt.

"Catherine, my sympathies to you, also. Your brother and his wife were wonderful people. I enjoyed their friendship."

Catherine nodded her thanks, set out tea and cookies, then sat down.

"If it's any consolation, Annalisa, your parents have provided well for you. They loved you very much, I know."

Annalisa wiped her eyes and tried to smile. "I know, too," she said softly.

"If you are ready, then, I will read the will." After he'd finished, Nathan switched to a conversational tone. "What this means, Annalisa, is that everything your parents owned they have left to you. The house is totally paid for, so there is no need for you to move. Your Aunt Catherine has been appointed your legal guardian until you reach the age of 21. If she agrees to live with you during this time..." (at this point, the lawyer looked at Catherine, who nodded her agreement) "she is to receive a small monthly compensation and adequate household allowance, which are both scheduled to come out of their IRA. Catherine has the legal right to make all decisions about the home, its contents, and financial resources until you reach the legal age of twenty-one. Then Catherine's duties will terminate."

Catherine asked, "Is there enough in the IRA? What about property taxes and home maintenance?"

"If we don't have a recession, there should be an adequate amount. You will have to budget all the bills and plan for the annual property taxes," Nathan replied.

Catherine nodded. "Being a contractor, my brother kept the home in good repair. So I do not expect any upkeep bills for a few years."

Annalisa thought of the frequent times her Dad worked on the house or yard, making repairs here and there. She burst into tears again. Catherine put her arm around her.

"It's hard to think I won't see Daddy working around the house anymore," she said between her sobs. "I used to enjoy bringing him a glass of lemonade or helping him with his work in some way."

Nathan waited patiently until Annalisa regained control and sat up straighter in her chair.

She lifted her chin in determination and looked at Catherine. "I can help with monthly bills. Daddy showed me how to write a check."

"They've also arranged for a monthly pension to be automatically deposited into a special account for Annalisa," Nathan continued. "Life insurance policies will go into the IRA."

Annalisa grabbed a tissue and wiped her eyes. All this boggled her mind, but she thought *What a blessing to have such loving parents! They've provided for all my needs.* In spite of her grief, it gave her a warm feeling.

"Do you have any other questions?" Nathan looked at each one in turn.

"How do we get my parents' bodies back from Ecuador? Is there a cemetery plot for the bodies? If not, how do I get one? Where do we purchase a grave stone?"

"Annalisa, you are an intelligent young lady to think of all the questions that need to be answered. Your parents would be very proud of you."

Annalisa smiled a little and looked at her lap. "Thank you, Sir."

"However, these are questions the mortician can better help you with. I assume your Pastor will go with you to the funeral home Monday to discuss arrangements. The funeral home will provide death certificates, too. You will also need to go to the license bureau to transfer the vehicles to your name, and to the bank to cancel their accounts."

She wrote that on a tablet under "A List of Things To Do."

"I'll make sure you get a deed to the house showing it is yours."

Nathan paused, still looking at her. Do you have any more questions?"

"No." Annalisa attempted a friendly smile. "Thank you for your help and guidance."

Nathan stood up. "I'll be in contact with you. Please call me if you have questions. Again, I am so sorry!" He shook hands warmly with both and then left.

"Well, that was encouraging," Aunt Catherine said, as she closed the door.

"Yes, my parents have provided well for me," Annalisa wiped her eyes again. *I do feel grateful, yet I would almost rather have died with them than be left without them.* They sat in silence for a time, then Catherine went to finish cleaning up the kitchen.

When she returned, she found Annalisa sitting on the couch with a large picture album in her hands. She sat beside her. Annalisa was crying again. "I can't stand it that I'll never see them again on this earth! I was already missing them, and then to hear they can't come back..."

"I know. This is extremely difficult to handle." Catherine's tears flowed freely, too.

"Look, here is their wedding picture, and you as maid of honor. They look so young."

Catherine wiped her eyes. "Yes, that was nearly 17 years ago."

"Oh, how I wish I could see them again!" wailed Annalisa.

"Yes, so do I." Catherine hugged her niece again. "Look. At the end of the book is one picture taken last month… Seventeen years of memories in one book."

The doorbell rang and Annalisa welcomed her best friend, Mary Lou, with a big hug. After they cried together for a few minutes, Annalisa led her over to the couch.

The next hour went quickly as the two mourners and friend paged through the book, remembering their loved ones, noticing how they'd changed through the years.

"As Nathan Page said, they sure were wonderful people. My big brother was always protective and good to me while I was growing up, and when they got married, I was thrilled to have Marcia for a sister-in-law."

"They were wonderful parents, too. They always let me know they loved me, even if they had to say "no" or if they had to discipline me. They would explain why, as best they could."

After Catherine served sandwiches, Mary Lou said goodnight. Annalisa sat with her aunt in the living room, watching the gathering darkness. Her heart felt dark like never before, and she sensed an ominous darkness taking over her mind. How could a good God take away her loving parents—especially when they were so committed to him, serving him by helping others?

Eventually, Catherine asked, "It's getting quite late, Annalisa. Are you tired?"

"Yes, I am. But I don't think I can sleep," she answered, dully.

"Same here, but I think we should try. Do you think you can handle going to church in the morning?"

"I might cry through the whole service."

"I might, too, but I'm sure everyone would understand. This is a tragedy for the whole church, with so many killed at once." She hesitated, watching Annalisa, then added quietly, "We should go. Perhaps all the grieving families can help support each other."

Annalisa put the album away. She wanted to think the church service would be comforting, but felt only anger at God. But she respected Catherine's wishes. "I guess," she said.

Catherine gave her niece a long hug. "Goodnight Dear."

They kissed each other on the cheek and went to their rooms.

Brenda's Regret

*M*eanwhile, across town, Brenda sat seething at the piano. She fought back the tears that stung her eyes. "I should think, now that I'm nearly sixteen, I should be allowed to make some of my own decisions!" she muttered under her breath.

She cringed as she heard her mother's voice from the doorway, "Get busy now, Brenda! You must practice more. Concert pianists usually practice about eight hours a day, I've heard."

She started with a scale, pounding the keys as quickly as she could go, up and down the keyboard again and again. It felt like she was punching a punching bag, and little by little her anger dissipated. Soon the strains of Chopin filled the air. The beauty of the music soothed her. *It's not that I don't like the music. I do. It's just that I wish I had time to make friends and do things other teenagers can do. I'm so lonely.*

Brenda hunted through her stack of music to find a Clementi Sonatina. It was too easy to work on now, when she was supposedly getting ready for a concert. But she felt the need to relax. She began to smile as the familiar melody poured from her fingers. As the song finished, she thought, *I wonder what Annalisa is doing today. She has so many friends. I suppose they are going to the mall, or a movie. What a lucky girl. She has everything going for her: looks, clothes, friends, grades, nice parents, lovely home.*

"Brenda, get back on task! You have only an hour to work on this before we have to go!"

Brenda sighed, and picked up her main concert number, Tchaikovsky's Concerto #1. The introduction had some loud chords and it gave her some gratification to play them as loud as possible. She played through the entire piece, then went back to work on a few tough spots with the metronome. The click, click, click, click helped the piece make sense when she matched the music with it. It also calmed her. *Maybe my life will start making sense if I just click, click, click, click....* It seemed a significant thought, but she knew she couldn't explain it to anyone.

As she gathered up the rest of the music she was to play at today's concert, Brenda's thoughts returned to Annalisa. *I wish I could get to know her better. She seems nice. But now I don't suppose she'll ever want to speak to me.* Brenda felt bad about the incident the other day. She hadn't meant it to come out that way.

Soon her mother's bossy voice broke into her reverie. "Brenda, it's time to get ready now. Hurry up or we'll be late for the Garden Club meeting. They want you to play before dinner."

Brenda sighed, got up and walked past her mother without looking at her. In her bedroom, she glanced in the mirror. *Oh well. Why would Annalisa want to be friends with me, anyway? I'm ugly and fat. I sure wouldn't want her to see me in these clothes. She's always dressed so nice.* Brenda looked at the clothes her mother had laid out for her to wear for the concert and stuck out her tongue. *They look like old lady clothes.* She repeated the words she had told herself as they left the store, "It's useless to argue." She put them on and tried to do something decent with her hair. *That's hopeless. I look like a gaudy scarecrow!*

In the car, Brenda tuned out her mother's chatter about the rich ladies in the Garden Club and how she was 'making connections.'

Brenda thought back to the 'incident' with Annalisa. They were both in English class—her favorite subject. The teacher handed back the tests they'd taken a couple of days earlier. *I knew I didn't do well, but I didn't think it would be that bad! If only Mom had let me stop practicing earlier, I could have studied more.* Brenda clenched her fists. She felt like putting her fingers in her ears so she didn't have to hear her mother's monologue about being a concert pianist, but knew that would bring her mother's anger down upon her again.

I never get D's! I couldn't believe my eyes. I thought at least I'd done well on the essay at the end. Sure enough, teacher had written "Good job" next to it. Just as I started to feel a little better, teacher told us, "I'm pleased that several of you did quite well on your essay question. I would like one who did especially well to come up and read her essay."

My heart started to beat faster with hope. But her next word shot me down.

"Annalisa... please." The teacher had smiled at Annalisa, who got up and read her essay.

I was so mad! Can't anything go right for me? Brenda's eyes had fogged up as she'd tried to leave the room quickly after class. She didn't want to break down in front of everyone. *I didn't plan to hurt Annalisa, but suddenly she was in my way and I bumped into her without seeing her. When I realized who it was, I reacted without thinking and said, "Get out of my way, Smarty Pants." Then I ran into the bathroom and bawled.*

Their car pulled up to an exquisite house with neat landscaping. Several cars were already parked in the circular driveway. Brenda's mother hurried her inside and greeted the hostess. "I do hope we're not late."

"Oh no, you're right on time," an elegantly dressed lady said. "Some of the ladies came early to plan our Christmas party."

Brenda held her breath, hoping her mother wouldn't volunteer her to play for that, also. She felt thankful that another lady captured the hostess's attention right at that moment. Soon the hostess welcomed the room full of fashionable ladies, then introduced Brenda, who played her pieces by rote memory. The clapping didn't even gratify her. She was just glad it was over.

Brenda waited, trying to disappear into the background, while her mother graciously accepted the compliments of the gushing ladies, and ate cookies with coffee. Finally, her mother ushered her out the door to the car. "You could have at least smiled at the ladies," her mother said. "How do you expect your audiences to invite you back if you aren't pleasant to them?"

As her mother went on and on about how a concert pianist should behave, Brenda looked out the window without seeing. *Always complaining. Never encouraging. I'm never good enough...* A sob escaped her throat as she thought, *I wish Dad was here.*

When they reached their house, Brenda burst out of the car almost before it stopped, ran into her room, and slammed the door. She stayed there until she heard her mother go to bed, then she snuck out to the kitchen to find something to eat.

3

A Cry in The Night

*"O Lord my God, I call for help by day;
I cry out in the night before thee." Psalm 88:1.*

Annalisa had cried herself to sleep that first night after hearing the terrible news. A couple hours later she awoke, listening. *It sounds like someone crying... is it Mom?*

As the sleep cleared from her brain she thought of the nightmare … then remembered it wasn't a nightmare. *Of course! It couldn't be Mom crying. Pastor Brady said my parents have been killed!* She rubbed her chest, half expecting to feel a hole where the pain was. She crept quietly into the guest bedroom. Great sobs came from the bed.

Annalisa stepped to the bedside and laid a hand gently on her aunt's shoulder. "Aunt Catherine?" Her aunt turned and looked at her, placing her hand over Annalisa's.

Annalisa noticed her aunt's eyes were red and swollen. "Would you like me to stay here with you?"

Catherine choked and coughed as she wiped her eyes. Between sobs, she said, "Yes, Dear. Lay down here and we'll cuddle." She lifted the side of the blanket up and Annalisa crawled in next to her. They hugged each other tight.

"Are you crying because you're sad?"

"Yes, I miss my brother and sister-in-law. I hate the thought of never seeing them again on this earth. I'm also scared. I love you so much and want to take good care of you, but this is a big responsibility and I'm afraid I might not do it right. I've never had a daughter."

"Jesus will help you. And I will try to be good. I'm so grateful you are here."

Catherine soon quit sobbing and lay still. "Thank you, that's encouraging."

Annalisa felt comforted at both the presence and the words of her aunt. But she wondered, *Will Jesus really help her? Why did I say that? If Jesus allowed my parents to be killed, can I trust him to help Aunt Catherine?*

As if reading her thoughts, Catherine said, "You're right. I know He will help me."

Catherine gave another hug. They listened to the peaceful silence for several minutes.

"Does it hurt—like a hole in your chest?" Annalisa asked. "Mine does."

"Yes. That's because we love them so much. But remember, it is better to have had someone to love, even though it hurts after they're gone, than if we'd never had anyone to love at all. Unlike many people, we have a lot of happy memories of them."

"I know."

"And like I said before, we are not like those who have no hope. Jesus will be with us and we will see them again in Heaven. We'll just have to remember the happy memories and go on to live the types of lives that are pleasing to God. That would please them, too."

Catherine brushed Annalisa's hair away from her face. "Would you like to pray the Lord's Prayer together?" she asked.

Annalisa was silent. She wanted to believe. Maybe she could choose to believe or choose to be bitter. Finally she answered. "Yes, but let's do it slowly, so we can think what it means. As they prayed slowly, Annalisa began to feel comforted by the fact that God was her loving heavenly Father. She didn't understand why things like this happen, but she wanted God's will to be done and for his kingdom to grow and flourish on earth. She also felt reassured God would provide her daily physical needs and emotional strength. *But Lord, I miss them so!*

As if understanding what she was thinking, Aunt Catherine quoted a Bible verse: "Lo, I am with you always, even to the end of the age," (Mt.28:20, NKJV). Soon it felt to Annalisa almost as if an angel was covering them with a warm blanket of peace. They both fell asleep until morning.

The next morning, Annalisa and Catherine got ready for church as was usual on Sundays.

"Aunt Catherine, I felt like a blanket of peace covered us as we slept. Did you?"

"Yes, after we cried and talked and cuddled, I felt God's peace, also."

"I'd heard of the peace that passes understanding," added Annalisa, "but never really understood it until now."

Catherine gave her a little hug. "However, it will still be difficult to see people who won't know what to say. Let's pray the Lord will help us."

After praying, they walked the three blocks to Gardenia's Hope Community Church in the crisp September air. Trees already started to turn fall colors of orange and yellow and brown. The scene was comforting to Annalisa in spite of the pain, which continued in her chest, and the longing for her parents' presence. *Why Lord? They went on this trip to serve you. If you are a God of love, you must have a good reason. Will you tell me why you allowed them to be killed?*

"Here we are. Do you need my hankie, Dear?"

"Thanks." Annalisa quickly wiped her eyes as they started up the steps. As they went through the door, it seemed as if everyone stopped talking and stared at her. Her Sunday School teacher came over and hugged her in a long comforting hug. Then the youth group leaders were there hugging her and expressing sympathy. She noticed a couple others, who had met Catherine the previous two Sundays or on previous visits, expressing their sympathy to Catherine.

Mary Lou's hug especially comforted Annalisa. She'd been her best friend since kindergarten. She went with them into the sanctuary and sat by her. After the congregation had sung the first hymn and sat down, Pastor Brady said, "I have some very sad news. Some of you have already heard it, but many haven't. The entire mission team, which has been ministering in Ecuador for the past two weeks, was killed in a plane crash early Saturday while on their way home. All twenty-two people were killed." Pastor Brady choked on a sob.

Annalisa could feel the shock wave go through the church as the news registered. She heard people gasp or say "Oh no!" and others whispered and murmured. Some burst into tears.

Pastor continued: "We aren't sure exactly when or how services will be conducted, since the bodies are still in Ecuador, but will get that news to you by email and radio within a few days. Now let's all pray together."

After praying with the congregation for friends and family of the deceased, the Pastor said, "I would like to invite all family members of the deceased who are present to meet with me in the prayer room after the service for a group prayer. Praying together is one of the ways we can bear each other's burdens. Of course, if it becomes too emotional for you to sit through the service, you may go there at any time; it is the same room that is called the cry room."

Annalisa felt in a daze most of the service. When she looked at her aunt, she sensed she felt the same way. She was vaguely aware that the Pastor's sermon was about hope in the middle of tragedy and how "God's ways are sometimes beyond understanding. This is where trust and faith comes in." One song stood out as comforting: "Think About His Love." *His grace will see us through,* she thought. Now and then, she saw someone get up, weeping, and go to the cry room. Others, like them, quietly wept while staying in the sanctuary. Toward the end of the last hymn, Catherine nudged her and motioned to go to the prayer room for the meeting. As they reached the prayer room door, a man Annalisa recognized as a local handyman held it open for them. She noticed his eyes were red, as many others were also.

Soon Pastor Brady joined the group. "Let's hold hands and pray together," he said. Pastor Brady led them first in The Lord's Prayer, slowly enunciating each phrase. Then he said, "Lord Jesus, we thank you for giving us that prayer. Thank you also for giving us the Holy Spirit to help us pray when we can't find the words. You know we are all hurting here. Please comfort us. Please draw us nearer to you so we can receive the grace that you give, which enables us to get through grief. Guide us and direct us in the coming days when we need to make so many decisions. This can be so hard when we are in turmoil emotionally. Help each of us to have other loved ones to give us support. Thank you that your Word teaches that God can use evil for good. We pray you will somehow use this tragedy for good, as you did for Joseph in Genesis 50. Thank you for your promise to be with us continually. In Jesus' name. Amen."

After the prayer, Pastor Brady asked everyone to say their names for the benefit of a few who were not acquainted with each other. "It would be nice if you folks can be a support for each other." After they did this, he assured them he would be in touch with each of them, then, "Goodbye for now and God bless you."

After he left, some stayed in the prayer room to talk with each other.

Several people waited in the lobby to hug and sympathize with the bereaved people. Several friends from youth group greeted Annalisa. Mary Lou hugged her again with tears flowing down her cheeks and said, "Oh, Annalisa, I love you so much. I'm so sorry this happened!"

After Catherine and Annalisa had descended the outside steps, Annalisa suddenly tripped over a small buckle in the sidewalk. Two young men caught her just in time to keep her from hitting face first on the concrete walk. Annalisa burst into tears, and was helped by the two young men to a bench. She was crying so hard, she didn't recognize them at first. Catherine rushed up and sat beside her.

"Are you all right? Did you get hurt?" they all asked.

As soon as she regained control, she said, "I'm all right. It just scared me. I thought I would hit the sidewalk with my face." She looked at the two young men. "Thank you for catching me, Todd and Travis. This is my Aunt Catherine."

The two young men greeted Catherine and shook her hand. "We go to the same school as Annalisa and are also in youth group," Todd said to Catherine. Then he turned to Annalisa. "We are so sorry about your parents' deaths. We know you'll be grieving for a long time and we would like to be your friends … just to be available if you need a friend to talk to."

Annalisa didn't know what to say. She just looked from one to the other. It did her heart good to know someone wanted to help her.

Travis handed her a small brochure. "This tells about a grief support group we are part of, which meets at the school each week. We'd love to have you join us when you are able. Also, maybe we could help with the things your father did at your home. Just two guys who could be like your older brothers."

Todd handed her a note. "These are our phone numbers. Call us whenever you need help, need to talk, or just need a friend close by." Annalisa tried unsuccessfully to smile, but nodded and took the note.

When they had gone, Catherine said, "I'm sure glad those young men caught you! You could have been seriously hurt!" Annalisa still felt stunned. It scared her to think what might have happened if they had not been at just the right place and at just the right time to catch her.

"I have the impression they could be nice friends for you," Catherine said, brushing Annalisa's hair out of her eyes. Annalisa just nodded.

"Are you ready to go home now?" Catherine asked.

Annalisa nodded again and stood up.

Once in the door of the empty house, Annalisa went to her room, collapsed in a heap on her bed and wept until finally her aunt said, "Honey, please, you need to eat something." So she came to the table and ate some of the prepared casserole a neighbor had brought over.

"Thanks, Aunty. I do feel a little better now."

Soon the doorbell rang and Catherine let Pastor Brady in. After greeting her, he came into the kitchen. "Hello, Annalisa. I was glad to see you two in church. It was brave of you to come in the midst of the emotional turmoil I'm assuming you are going through."

"Thank you, Pastor Brady." Annalisa wiped her eyes. "It helped to get some hugs. I liked the prayer session afterward, and I love that song, "Think About His Love."

"I won't take much of your time, but we need to decide a couple things about the funeral."

Catherine pointed to a chair and Pastor sat down. "Yes, but since they went to Heaven, is it all right to call it something else other than a funeral? Funeral sounds so depressing."

Pastor nodded to Catherine. "I agree. Some people call it a memorial service, and others a celebration of life."

"How about a 'Home-going Service?' Annalisa asked, quietly.

Pastor Brady looked thoughtfully at Annalisa. "I like that. Sounds good."

"Have you talked to everyone else? Will it be a joint service?" Catherine asked.

"Yes, most agree that a joint service for those who were members of our church is best. Three of the couples were from other churches and will have their own services. Our joint service will be for seven couples and two single persons."

"I think a joint service will be nice," Annalisa said. "It will draw the church together and feel more supportive. Besides, most of the people who would go to one service would want to go to the others, also. Maybe the other churches should have theirs on a different day?"

"That is thoughtful of you, Annalisa," Pastor Brady said. "I suggest we have the service later this week, rather than waiting. Shipping the bodies home will take at least two weeks. We could have a private burial service for each family later. Does that sound like a good plan?"

Catherine and Annalisa looked at each other, grabbed each other's hand, and nodded to the Pastor. Tears sprang to the eyes of both.

"I will ask the others if they feel comfortable calling it a Home-going Service. If not, is Celebration of Life or Memorial Service acceptable?" They nodded again. "How about this Friday for the joint service? That should give us time to plan what is needed."

"Yes, that is all right with us." Annalisa felt numb, like her brain had quit working.

"I would like you each to decide on a scripture and hymn for the service. They could be your favorites, or favorites of Marcia and Bob. I will come by in the morning about 9 a.m. and go with you to the mortuary. There we will make more decisions."

Pastor Brady prayed with them again, then said, "See you in the morning" and left.

Annalisa sat like a statue. She felt cold.

After the Pastor left, Catherine said, "Let's go for a walk, Annalisa. They say exercise helps people feel better. Then maybe we can take a nap."

The sight of the fall colors did cheer her up a bit. Annalisa began to feel warmer after putting on her coat and walking a ways. After a short nap, they spent the evening thinking and talking about scriptures and hymns to use. That night in the guest room bed, they talked of memories until they couldn't stay awake.

Brenda's Sickness

Brenda's late night supper didn't sit well. At midnight, she got up to the bathroom and vomited. *It's not surprising that mother doesn't seem to hear me, since she always sleeps soundly after taking sleeping pills.*

The rest of the night, Brenda slept fitfully, with snatches of dreams. One time she woke herself up screaming, *Daddy, come back!*

She lay there shaking and crying, remembering an argument in the dream. It had really happened years earlier. Brenda's mother had insisted on taking Brenda to the Garden Club's Fall Extravaganza to be on the program. "She's only five years old," her dad said. "She'll be scared with all those women fussing over her." As usual, her mother had her way. Brenda was terrified, but didn't dare disobey her mother; that would terrify her even more. Afterward, she had wet her pants and had cried all the way home.

That evening, her dad had tried to comfort her by holding her on his lap and reading her a story, but her mother interrupted in the middle of the story and insisted it was time for Brenda to practice piano. "Let her be," he'd said. "She's had a trying day."

I guess Daddy thought Mother would pull me in two if he tried to hold on to me. So he gave up, then he left the house, angry.

As Brenda reminisced about the dream/memory, she kept on crying and shaking. Soon she realized it wasn't just the memory. She was having chills and she ached all over. She ran to the bathroom with a sudden urge of diarrhea. After cleaning herself up, she took aspirin for the aching, but immediately threw up again. Back in bed, she rolled up in the covers and an extra blanket and cried herself to sleep.

Fitful dreams continued … mostly snatches of her parents fighting.

The next time Brenda fully woke up, she was in the hospital. A bag of fluid was hanging over her with one end in her arm. *How did I get here? And why?* She looked around and saw a cord tied to the railing that had a button and said "call." She pushed it and soon a nurse came in.

"Hello Brenda. I'm your nurse, Miranda. What can I do for you?"

"What happened? Why am I here? And how did I get here?"

"Your mother brought you in yesterday evening. You had a fever of 105 and were delirious. We are still trying to figure out why. How much do you remember?"

"Late Saturday night, I ate a snack and went to bed. I got up and vomited about midnight. Then I woke up later with bad dreams, and felt so cold and ached all over. I had diarrhea, too."

The nurse checked her temperature and blood pressure. "What did you have for your bedtime snack?"

"I think it was tuna fish. It tasted funny, though."

"Hmm. How do you feel now?" Nurse Miranda straightened her bed and fluffed her pillows a bit.

"My stomach still hurts. And I still ache a little, but not as bad as before. What day is it?"

"It is Monday afternoon."

"It wasn't even daylight on Sunday the last I knew."

"Yes, you've been a very sick girl. They pumped your stomach thinking you might have food poisoning. That's probably why your stomach hurts now. Do you know how old the tuna fish was?"

Brenda's mother entered the room. "What tuna fish?"

The nurse turned to her. "Oh, hello Mrs. Polanski. Brenda says she ate tuna fish late Saturday evening. How old was it?"

"Why, I don't remember. I forgot it was in there. It must have been at least a week old!"

Nurse Miranda made a note on the chart, then said, "Excuse me, please," and left the room.

Brenda watched her mother nervously sit down on the chair. She looked worn out. "I'm glad you're awake," her mother said, not quite looking at her. "I didn't know what to think. I thought you were sleeping when I went to work yesterday morning, and then when I came home, I found you hot and shaking and delirious, so I took you right down to the hospital."

Brenda wasn't sure how to respond. "Thanks."

"It's sure too bad you are losing all this practice time."

Brenda groaned and turned her face away.

Her mother spoke again. "I hope you don't mind, but I have to get back to work. They will take good care of you here. They said it might be a couple more days before you can go home."

Brenda felt almost relieved. "Mother, would you please do something for me?"

"What?"

"Bring me my school books and find out what assignments I'm missing?"

"OK, yes, I can do that."

Brenda went back to sleep after her mother left, and felt some better after her nap. By the time her mother was off work and brought the books, she felt well enough to study a little.

Thursday evening she was discharged from the hospital with a diagnosis of food poisoning complicated by influenza and dehydration. "You're very weak from this ordeal," the doctor said. "I recommend you stay home from school all next week, but the school counselor can bring your schoolwork and help you catch up. I will talk to her."

It would have been a relaxing time if it weren't for the fact her mother still expected her to practice. But Brenda didn't mind too much. Since the Doctor had told her mother Brenda had to rest, she only insisted on half the usual amount of time spent practicing and let her do it in segments. Brenda liked the music itself, and her anger seemed to be gone. In fact, as far as her emotions were concerned, well, they seemed to be numb. She felt almost like an orphan and had decided she had to refuse to feel anything. It hurt too much to feel.

Mrs. Hoffman, the school counselor, came on the following Monday morning to pick up her assignments and bring new ones, and did the same each day. At first Brenda didn't say much, but by the end of the week she eagerly looked forward to the warmth of Mrs. Hoffman's visits.

"You are a good student, Brenda. It seems you are actually doing better sick than you normally do."

"That's because the Dr. told my mother I need to rest, so she's not making me practice piano as much right now. So I have more time to study."

"How much do you usually practice?"

"Mother says I need to practice four hours a day."

"What!" Mrs. Hoffman looked shocked. "My children are expected to practice half an hour a day. Of course, they are younger, but still..."

Brenda felt a flash of jealousy. *What would it be like to be her daughter?* "Mother thinks I'm going to be a concert pianist. In the summer when there's no school, she insists I practice eight hours a day." Brenda said, with a sigh of resignation.

Mrs. Hoffman's eyes flashed. She quickly looked out the window. When she looked back, her eyes had a soft look in them. "In spite of that, you've been maintaining a B average in your schoolwork. That's wonderful. You are a remarkable girl."

Brenda flushed with pleasure. It was nice to receive a compliment.

"How do you feel about your mother's plan for you to become a concert pianist?"

It was Brenda's turn for her eyes to flash with anger. "I don't want to! I don't like to show off like she thinks I should. I mean, I like the music, but I want to have time for other things, too. I want to do well in my schoolwork. I want to be able to choose my own life's work. I want to have friends and take part in other activities." By this time she was crying.

"Of course you do," Mrs. Hoffman said, soothingly, touching her hand. "You're a normal girl." She sat quietly for a moment while Brenda blew her nose. "Tell you what, how about if we get together and talk once a week or more. Maybe it will help you feel better."

Brenda sniffed and looked at Mrs. Hoffman. "I'd like that."

"You are planning to return to school Monday, right?"

Brenda nodded.

"Do you want to eat lunch with me?"

Brenda smiled. "Oh yes, that would be great."

"All right. You pick up your lunch and then come right to my office and we'll talk and eat together. Then we'll decide if that's the best time each week to meet. Now I better go so you can do some homework before your mother gets home."

"Thank you. Bye."

5

Arrangements

$\mathcal{M}$onday morning, Pastor Brady drove Catherine and Annalisa to the Gardenia funeral home. "I'll be along in a bit. I have to take this phone call first."

While Catherine used the rest room, Annalisa approached the office. She said in a shaky voice, "I'm Annalisa Schuiteman. Could I speak to the mortician?"

"One moment please." The receptionist stepped into an adjoining room. A man came out.

"Hello, I'm William Bates, the mortician, aka funeral director, how may I help you?"

"Sir, my parents died..." She burst into tears. Before she could recover, Pastor Brady was at her side and finished her sentence... "in a plane crash in Ecuador. We want to bring their bodies home and arrange for their burials."

"Are they part of the group that was on the mission trip?" Mr. Bates asked. He looked from Pastor Brady to Annalisa.

Annalisa nodded.

"The Embassy of Ecuador has already contacted us," Mr. Bates informed them, "and told us about the crash. They found the plane and the bodies, with identification on some of them. They will embalm the bodies, place them in caskets, and fly them to the United States. Most likely they'll arrive in Sioux City or Sioux Falls. I'll go to the airport, claim them and return them to Gardenia. I'll let you know when they arrive. It will take two weeks or more." He looked at Annalisa with soft eyes. "My sympathy goes out to you for the loss of your parents, Annalisa."

Annalisa nodded, then looked down the hall. "This is my Aunt Catherine," Annalisa said to Mr. Bates, when her aunt joined them. "She lives with me, now. My dad was her brother."

Mr. Bates shook Catherine's hand and said warmly, "May I express my sympathy in the loss of your brother and sister-in-law."

"Thank you. I'm glad to meet you, but not glad of the reason for doing so."

Mr. Bates gestured toward an open room. "Let's all sit down in this room across the hall." Annalisa and her Aunt Catherine and Pastor Brady soon were seated in comfortable chairs near a large table.

Mr. Bates looked at Catherine and Annalisa. "Do you have other family members?"

"No. I am an only child." *An orphan.* Annalisa felt weak-kneed when she realized--- *That's right, I'm an orphan now. How will I manage without Mom's and Dad's advice and love and care? She lifted a shaky hand to her mouth.* The realization hit hard, and she started sniffling again.

"My grandparents died a few years ago, and my dad was my aunt's only sibling."

"It's good you have each other, at least."

"Yes, I'm thankful for my aunt." She took Catherine's hand and squeezed it. "My parents left for the mission trip two weeks ago. On Saturday, I learned about the plane crash."

Mr. Bates nodded. "As did eleven other families in the area. Three of the couples are from the neighboring towns, so other funeral homes will handle those. We will handle the other seven couples plus the two unmarried people."

What a lot of hurting people, Annalisa thought.

He continued. "I will make all the necessary arrangements to have the bodies returned to the United States. The Embassy person said they will require dental records since there was a fire when the plane struck the mountain. I'll need the name of your parent's dentist so their records can be faxed to the embassy. Such a search, and what needs to be done there, will probably take about two weeks, they said."

Annalisa began to cry. "Do you mean my parents' bodies may be so damaged that I may not recognize them?"

"I'm afraid so. Since they were in a plane crash there probably isn't much I can do to make them look like you remember them. I would suggest that we not open the caskets for viewing. You'll want to remember how they looked when they left."

Pastor Brady spoke up. "We have decided to do a joint service for the sixteen who attended our church. We plan to do it this week on Friday, and then have private burial services for each family when the bodies are ready."

Mr. Bates nodded. "Yes, that is wise. Would you like us to provide bulletins for the service or does your church have those?"

"We have a few choices, but yours are more appealing. We'll print them at the church."

"I'd suggest individual bulletins for each couple, even though it is a joint service," Mr. Bates said. "This is often quite meaningful to a family." They all nodded, and Annalisa felt relieved.

"We plan to call it a Home-going Service, since they were all Christians and are going home to Heaven," Pastor Brady added.

"We want the service to be a celebration of their lives, and how they sought to serve Jesus," Annalisa added.

Mr. Bates nodded. "Good idea. Now would you ladies like to choose a bulletin cover from this book?"

Annalisa and Catherine looked together and chose one with a red rose and a cross on it. They pointed it out to Pastor Brady and he nodded, giving 'thumbs up.'

"Did your parents have a cemetery lot?" Mr. Bates asked.

"I don't know. That was my next question." Annalisa looked at Catherine, who shrugged.

"One moment. I'll call the Memorial Gardens Cemetery here in Gardenia." Mr. Bates dialed his cell phone and quickly obtained the information. "Yes, they have purchased cemetery plots already. You can go to Memorial Monuments to have a memorial stone carved."

"I like the bulletin you chose," said Pastor Brady. "We can put the obituary of one parent on the inside, the other on the back, and the program of the service on the other inside page, or else both parents on the inside pages and program on the back."

"I like the second suggestion best," Annalisa said.

Annalisa's head was spinning. *So many details to plan— even for one funeral. And now there are 22 dead all at once!* She looked at Pastor Brady sympathetically. *Nine families are a lot to minister to in one week.*

William Bates turned to the others. "I believe that is all the information I need except for choosing the pallbearers for the graveside service. Do you want to do that now, or should we wait until the bodies arrive?"

Annalisa seemed to hear the words through a fog and didn't answer. She heard Catherine say, "We might as well choose them now."

"I'll need twelve names from you since we use six persons per casket. You think about who you would like and bring me the list, then I'll contact them from your list. I'll let your Pastor know when all is ready here for the graveside service and then he'll decide with you on the date. We don't need to choose caskets since they will embalm them and send them in caskets."

Annalisa's heart ached. Her mind felt too foggy to think.

As they headed to the door to leave, Pastor Brady asked, "Would you please write a brief history of their lives for the memorial cards and for the Home-going Service bulletin and drop it off to me by Thursday am?"

"Yes, we will do that," Catherine nodded goodbye to Mr. Bates. "Thank you for your help."

On the way to the car Aunt Catherine looked at Annalisa and smiled slightly. "I am proud of you. You made it through that. When my parents died, I just dissolved into a puddle of tears and could not do a thing. Your Dad had to take care of all arrangements." She squeezed Annalisa's hand. "I'm glad you're my niece."

Annalisa's answering smile was sad, but showed appreciation for the compliment. "I'm glad you're my aunt," she answered.

After the Pastor dropped them off at home, they discussed the Home-going Service. They agreed to ask Pastor to speak on John 3:16 and Jeremiah 29:11 about God's love for his people. For music, they chose, "Blessed be the Name," and "Think About His Love."

During the three days before the Home-going Service, they first worked together on the history and took that to Pastor Brady. Then they sorted through sympathy cards, clothes, personal effects, pictures and papers. They shared memories and cried together. Often visitors came, leaving cards or food and offers "to help."

"I have no idea what to say when people offer to help," Annalisa said to Aunt Catherine after one visit. "What can they do? Bring my parents back?"

Aunt Catherine put a hand on her arm. "I'm sure they wish they could. They would just like to comfort you in some small way."

Annalisa sighed. "Yeah, I know. I'd rather they'd just give me a hug."

"I know. I feel the same way. It's especially hard if I don't even know the person."

The night before the Home-going Service, Annalisa stared at the stars. *Where's heaven, God? Are they up there somewhere? Why can't you send them back to me?* Tears ran down her cheeks. She finally got into bed and curled up into a fetal position, weeping until daybreak.

Chapter

6

The Home-going Service

On Friday, Annalisa put on a soft, blue dress with a gathered skirt. With her blonde hair combed and shoes polished she was ready for the service.

"You certainly look pretty," Catherine said.

"Thank you. This was my Daddy's favorite outfit. He smiled every time I wore this dress. Mom had helped me pick it out."

"It is appropriate, then, to wear it for their Home-going service."

"You look nice too, Aunt Catherine. I'm grateful that you're here. I don't know what I'd do if I had to face this alone."

"You are a help to me, too, my dear. I miss my brother and sister-in-law very much, just as you miss your parents. It made me feel better the last few evenings to have you with me to share pictures and memories of them."

"Yes, me too. But for some reason, knowing they are gone hurts more this morning."

"That's probably because the truth of their deaths has fully reached your heart. Oh, by the way, Mary Lou called while you were in the shower. She'll meet us there for the prayer meeting and she and her parents will sit with us through the service." Catherine gave Annalisa a hug. "Well, we better start for the church. Since we are going to walk, it will take about 10 minutes."

Those closest to the deceased met a half hour early for prayer with the Pastor. Mary Lou met Annalisa and hugged her before they went in to the prayer room.

"… and so, Lord, we thank you that you promised to be with us always. Help all these bereaved ones to feel your comforting love. Please work through this tragedy for good, somehow, and may your name be glorified."

"Amen" several people responded.

Gardenia Community Church was packed. It seemed the whole town was related to one or the other of the seven couples, or to Phyllis Vander Broek or Emil Warner, all of whom had died in the crash. The ushers had divided the church into nine sections so each group of survivors could sit together. They helped other visitors decide where they preferred to sit.

When everyone was seated, Pastor Brady walked to the front of the church and began the service. "Dear friends, we do mourn the loss of our loved ones, but not as those who have no hope. We do have the hope of seeing them again in eternity. We are here to celebrate the lives of seven couples and two single persons of our church who passed from this life into eternity while returning from a mission trip to Ecuador. Twenty-two people in all were on that mission trip and died in that airplane when it crashed. Three of the couples were from neighboring towns. Their services will be next week. Please remember to pray for all the families who are mourning."

Pastor Brady bowed his head for a moment. His shoulders shook and his voice sounded husky when he began again.

"Those who were members of our church are: Pierre and Francine Le Beau, Juan and Juanita De La Vega, Ernst and Frieda Hess, Natalie and Jim Krautz, Tomas and Jin Lin, Bob and Marcia Schuiteman, Phyllis Vander Broek, Joseph and Sophia Vander Huis, and Emil Warner. The families of each have given me scriptures to use for a short message and songs we can sing between messages. Let's start by singing "Draw Me Nearer" which is a choice of the Le Beaus."

"I Am Thine O Lord ..." Annalisa looked around as she sang the familiar song. How could so many people be hurting so much all at once? Many were openly weeping and others had red eyes. She bowed her head and sought her quiet place of prayer. *Father, I'm grateful to you for letting me have my wonderful parents for fifteen years. I'll miss them so much. I don't understand why you would let them die when they served you so well. But they taught me you are holy and righteous, so you must know what you are doing, and I know you love me.*

When Pastor Brady had finished the messages for the other families of the deceased and the congregation had sung a song between each, he said, "Bob and Marcia Schuiteman also enjoyed serving the Lord and this mission trip was just one example of many where they gave of their time and talents to help others in many places. Other people have heard about Jesus and will have a better life because of them. Their daughter, Annalisa, and Bob's sister, Catherine, have requested a CD be played of "When God Ran" because it was Bob's favorite song. It illustrates how God yearns for relationship with each of us. Hopefully, each one of you can imagine your head on God's chest with him hugging you, as you listen."

He sat down on a stool while the song played, then stood again. "Annalisa has chosen John 3:16 and Jeremiah 29:11 for me to speak about. Many of you know the first by memory, so let's recite it together. "For God so loved the world that he gave his only begotten Son, that whoever believes in him shall not perish but have eternal life."

Annalisa felt touched by the strength of the recitation. She squeezed Mary Lou's hand.

Pastor Brady continued. "Her parents knew and loved the Lord and spent much time working on projects that reflected these two verses. To them, a mission trip was more than just a work project, it was an opportunity to carry out Jesus' commission to go into the entire world and teach others about Him." Annalisa felt grateful her aunt sat beside her.

"The second verse, Annalisa, I'd like to direct specifically to you. I know that, as a young girl, you may have many fears about getting along without your mother and father. But God has a good plan for your life. You chose Jeremiah 29:11 and it says, "For I know the plans I have for you," declares the Lord, "plans to prosper you and not to harm you, plans to give you hope and a future." Your parents fit into God's plan for their lives through obedience to what they believed God wanted them to do. They lived that plan as their way of serving God and their fellow man. God was glorified by what they did for Him. I'm sure they have prayed, while they raised you, that you would always fit into God's plan for your life. You can embrace that plan if you fully trust in God's love." Annalisa reached for her tissues. She felt like something was wrong with God's plan.

"Let us all now stand and sing a song which speaks of God's love for all people," said Pastor Brady: "Think About His Love." Then after the benediction, we will sing "Blessed Be The Name" which is a favorite of several of these bereaved families.

The relatives of each of the dead persons were dismissed in turn. The church served a lunch, but Annalisa didn't feel much like eating or talking. *I feel grateful for the service, God,* Annalisa prayed, *but this is hard. How can I believe this is a good plan? Please give me strength.*

"Aunt Catherine, do you mind if we go home right away?" She nodded. Annalisa hugged Mary Lou goodbye, and the two left the building clinging to each other, both wiping their eyes.

As they began to walk home, a cold wind came up. Todd and Travis drove their car up beside them. "Would you like a ride, ladies?" They both got in. Annalisa felt grateful for the ride.

Soon they reached her house and stopped in the driveway. "May we visit you tomorrow?" Todd asked. "Maybe we can bring you some sunshine."

Annalisa looked at Aunt Catherine, who said, "That would be nice. But how about if you give us a week—could you come on Saturday next week at 2 pm instead?"

They nodded, and she said, "Thank you for the ride, boys. It is colder than I thought, or I would have driven."

7

Mother's Plans

*B*renda couldn't stop thinking about what Mrs. Hoffman had said: "You are a remarkable girl." The pleasure of the compliment overwhelmed her, as if she'd never received one before. *Have I ever received a compliment? Not that I remember ...Oh yes, Dad told me I looked pretty in my new dress the first day of school. That was ten years ago. And when I showed him my poem in fifth grade, he said it was nice.*

Mrs. Hoffman had also called her a normal girl. That was reassuring. She'd begun to think she was some sort of freak, judging from the way people shied away from her. This seemed to have started shortly after the breakup of her parents when she was in Seventh grade.

Was their divorce my fault? How could I have prevented it? Maybe if I'd been more cooperative with Mother about practicing? Or maybe if I'd refused and just done what Dad wanted me to do?

Brenda decided she'd better put all this thinking out of her mind and get her homework done. If she procrastinated until her mother got home, she would have to get busy practicing piano and the homework would not get done.

She worked steadily on it for two hours, then ran to the piano just as her mother drove in the driveway.

"Oh good! You are practicing," her mother said, as she walked into the house. At least there would be a fair amount of peace if she did what her mother wanted. Soon she got lost in the music and it began to sooth the resentful feelings inside.

When they sat down to supper together, Brenda almost felt grateful to her mother. But the pleasant feelings were soon dashed when she heard her mother's plans.

"I was talking with the music director at the college— you know, Pere Marquette University right here in Gardenia, about you giving a concert there sometime," mother said. "They were hesitant, because of your age, but I convinced them to consider it. Mr. Shaw will consult with the rest of the music faculty and let us know."

Brenda felt her chest tighten up again."Mother, don't you think you should have asked first if I was interested in doing that?"

"Why of course you are. Why wouldn't you be? There could be up to 1500 students plus all those teachers to hear you. And many of those are international students who could take news of you home with them.This would be a wonderful opportunity for you to further establish your career as a concert pianist. Besides, it might help them decide to give you a music scholarship. You know we can't afford college otherwise."

Brenda contemplated that. Actually, she had dreamed of attending Pere Marquette University after high school. It was a good liberal arts college. But she had hoped to major in medicine, not in music. If she received a music scholarship, did she have to major in music?

Mother began clearing the table and signaled to her to help, then said, "Mr. Shaw's wife is a member of the Garden Club, so she has told him how well you play."

A compliment? Is mother giving me a compliment? I suppose she must think I play really well, or why would she try to set up concerts? Maybe I've been a little too critical of her? But still, I wish I had some say in my life's plans. Brenda shook her head, as if to clear the fog.

"Hurry up now with these dishes so you can finish practicing. You've only done an hour."

There was no use telling her she still had homework to do. That would have to wait until bedtime, when she would do it instead of sleep. No wonder she'd gotten sick. Oh well, she had all day tomorrow to catch up on it---except for her expected four hours of practice.

"By the way, I'm taking you to French Town tomorrow. They have a flea market going on all day and I talked them into letting you play piano in the background. It will enhance their sales. I told them we could be there by 11 o'clock and you could play until it's over at 5."

"Mother! I've just been sick and you are expecting me to play for six hours when I should be working on my homework? And do I get to eat or go to the bathroom?"

"Well, of course that will take the place of your practice time at home. And you can do some of your homework in the car. It's an hour drive."

Brenda opened her mouth to say more, but her mother said, "That's enough complaining now. Mother knows best. Oh, and I also lined up a concert for you for the Kiwanis Club on the fifth Friday in October."

Brenda groaned. "But that's homecoming; I wanted to go to the game!"

"Oh tut tut. Concert pianists don't have time for games. You need to focus on your single-minded goal."

Brenda's eyes filled with tears, but she turned away quickly. If her mother saw, she would call her a crybaby as she had in the past. She went quickly to her room where she could close the door and cry. *It's not fair! Why can't I even have some fun like others my age? If I can't do any of the normal teenage activities, how can I ever make friends?* Presently her mother knocked on the door and ordered her to get to the piano, pronto.

The next day seemed never to end. Brenda was exhausted when she finished, yet it didn't seem as if anyone had even listened to her play. She fell asleep in the car on the way home.

8

Someone to Listen

They watched the boys drive away in their yellow jeep, then turned to each other. Annalisa's eyes glistened with tears as she said softly, "That was nice." They walked into the house and she shut the door.

"I'm so exhausted, Aunt Catherine. I think I'll take a nap."

"Good idea. I will also. A service like that can be exhausting because of our raw grief."

After a long nap, Annalisa felt refreshed and wanting company. She found her aunt in the living room.

"It was nice of the boys to give us a ride home," said Aunt Catherine. "I think they will be good friends for you. Have you seen them at school before?"

"Yes, but I haven't talked to them personally before last Sunday when they caught me, except when they asked me if my parents had gone with the mission team."

"Oh? When was that?"

"The day my parents left. You arrived later that day before I came home from school."

"Yes, I remember. Let's go have some hot chocolate." They went to the kitchen and Catherine turned on the burner under the tea kettle. "So they knew your parents were going?"

"Yes, they must have heard it at church. I have seen them at church, and also at youth group. But they are older and I was afraid I'd be too forward if I went up to them to talk."

"I don't imagine you were too happy that day. I think you told me you had tried to talk your parents into not going on this mission trip?" Both sat down at the table after Catherine prepared cups of hot chocolate.

"Right. I had the feeling something terrible was going to happen. I told my parents what I'd learned in school---that there were cannibals in Ecuador and the roads were narrow and in poor condition. Also, the air at that altitude is so thin; airplanes have trouble gaining enough altitude to fly over the mountains. I told them their plane might crash, and kill all of them and that I didn't want to lose them." By this time, tears cascaded down Annalisa's cheeks. She started sobbing. "They told me 'just trust God' and that they wanted to tell the people about Jesus."

Aunt Catherine gently patted Annalisa's hand on the table. They sat silently for a few minutes. Finally Catherine said, "I suppose it feels like God let you down, but he is still trust-worthy. I'm hurting, too, but I don't think God makes mistakes. And I don't believe my brother and sister-in-law heard wrong. I believe God wanted them to go to Ecuador. When we get to Heaven, we will understand why it happened this way, but for now--- we do need to trust that God loves us and does what is best."

"Did God make the plane crash?"

"No, Dear. God does not cause evil to happen. Evil took hold of the world in the Garden of Eden because of disobedience of humanity. It's like Adam and Eve gave the dominion of earth to Satan when they disobeyed God."

"What's dominion?" Annalisa asked.

"Power or control. God had put Adam and Eve in charge, but they let Satan take over. Satan is at the root of all evil, often working through people. However, Genesis 50:20 says that God can use evil for good. And Romans 8:28..."

"I know that one. 'all that happens to us is working for good if we love God and are fitting into his plans.'"

"Yes, that is the Living Bible version of it," Catherine said.

Annalisa drank her hot chocolate thoughtfully.

"I guess Mom and Dad received good out of the crash because they're in heaven now?"

"Yes, we can be sure of that because they did love God and were fitting into his plans."

"So we need to believe he will work it out for our good, also?"

"Yes." Aunt Catherine wiped her eyes with her handkerchief.

Then she got up and put a prepared casserole in the microwave before asking, "Can you tell me more about the day they left? And what happened between you and Brenda?"

That day seems so long ago now. I thought I'd see them again after two weeks. "I rode with them to church at 7 a.m.," she told her aunt. "Most of the group was already there, standing around talking. The weather felt like summer instead of September 3rd. Some of them greeted me, and Mom and Dad introduced me to the ones I didn't know. They always seemed so happy to introduce me, as if they were proud of me and so happy to have me for a daughter." Her eyes filled with tears again.

Catherine dished up the casserole and put plates on the table.

Annalisa wiped her eyes and continued. "After our good-byes, I shouldered my back pack and walked toward school. I started crying, leaned against a tree, and thought, *"What if the plane crashes? What if the people in Ecuador become angry and attack and kill my parents?* I thought of the many things that could go wrong and I was so scared. I remember telling God, *I'm glad Aunt Catherine is staying with me, but I feel so alone with my parents going to Ecuador. Please God, be with me and keep us all safe. Bring us back together in two weeks.*

She paused so Catherine could pray the table prayer. They began eating. Then Catherine said, "Go on," and continued to listen attentively.

Annalisa continued: "I'd dried my tears by the time I'd arrived at the Gardenia high school block. There, I was greeted by several friends, including my best friend, Mary Lou. We saw Todd and Travis nearby. I knew them a little from youth group. *Todd and Travis seem like nice guys*, I thought, *so considerate and kind. With their rugged good looks, it's a wonder they don't have girls hanging around them all the time. Yet, they don't.*"

"Todd had been combing his wavy blond hair beside his Jeep when he caught sight of me. I saw him nudge the darker-haired Travis and heard him say. "Here she is." Both approached me, looking concerned."

"Did your parents leave on the mission trip this morning?"

"Yes, just a few minutes ago," I said.

"Are you okay?" Todd asked. I nodded, although my eyes filled with tears. Travis put his arm around my shoulder and gave me a slight squeeze.

"Don't worry. All will be well," he said.

"I believed him. I mean, it was so strange—one minute I felt awful inside and the next, after their concerned words and the shoulder-squeeze, I felt like everything would be okay eventually. I smiled at them and said, "Thanks, guys. I'll see you at youth group, right?" Todd and Travis nodded and gave a little wave. Then I ran to catch up to my girlfriends."

"Sometimes it doesn't take much to boost a person's spirits," Catherine said.

"Right. Then I said hello to some other friends, Betsy and Jenny Lynn. They asked me which of those good-looking guys is my boyfriend, but I said neither, because I'm too young to date—that they're just acquaintances from church. So then we just talked about how good they are at football. I'd heard Todd say at youth group that he'd like to coach high school football after college. Travis had said he'd rather go into social work or become a psychiatrist.

"What do you hope to do?" asked Catherine. She smiled, then finished her casserole.

"I think I'd like to teach. I have a great love for children," Annalisa said.

"Then we had to hurry into school because the bell was about to ring. I tripped on a step and got a bloody knee. Brenda was nearby and she blurted out as if announcing to the whole world, "The Princess has fallen!" Then she said to me, "Walk much? Or just read about it?""

Catherine looked sympathetic. "That's too bad. You were already feeling sad and scared, and then to have that happen...!"

"Yes, it was so rude to make fun of me and laugh when I got hurt."

"Did she know your knee was bleeding?"

Annalisa hesitated. "I'm not sure. I wonder.... Maybe she didn't know. I discovered it after she left. Maybe she was just trying to be funny, not mean."

Catherine smiled tenderly at Annalisa. "It's always best to put the best possible construction on a person's motives. They don't always intend to come across the way they do."

Annalisa nodded. She scooted her food around on her plate for a bit, thinking. "It didn't seem right that she call me Princess. That's—was—Daddy's pet name for me. It seemed like a loving nickname when he said it, but it sounded ugly from her."

Soon she continued, "The rest of the school day went okay, but on the way home, those feelings of fear for my parents' safety attacked me again, until I saw you."

She sat thoughtfully drinking her hot chocolate, wondering about Brenda. *Why has she been sarcastic to me so many times, ever since she moved here in seventh grade?*

Catherine spoke into her reverie. "Has something else happened between you and Brenda? I thought I overheard something when Mary Lou called you."

"Yes, it happened two weeks later, the day before Pastor gave us the bad news. We both have English class during first period. (It's my favorite subject.) The teacher handed back the tests we'd taken a couple days earlier, and I was happy to see I'd received an 'A'. Then she asked me to read my answer to the essay question aloud to the class."

"Why, congratulations! Good for you!" Catherine exclaimed.

"Thanks. Well, as I read it aloud, I was puzzled because I noticed Brenda giving me a dirty look. I couldn't figure out what she could be mad at me about."

"Maybe she was jealous because you were chosen to read the essay."

"Yeah, maybe. Anyway, as we were leaving class—I had just gotten out in the hallway when I realized I'd left my purse at my desk, so I turned around and wham! Brenda ran into me and knocked me down. All my stuff fell out of my hands and scattered all over the hall."

Annalisa rubbed her elbow to see if it still hurt. *It feels much better now.*

"Brenda said, in the meanest voice I've ever heard, "Watch where you're going, Smarty Pants!" She didn't stop to help or even see if I was okay. It took me so long to pick up my things that I was tardy for the next class and had to go get a tardy slip."

Catherine put her hand on Annalisa's as it lay on the table. "So you were having a rough time even before you got the bad news about your parents. I'm so sorry for you."

Tears ran down Annalisa's cheeks again. *It sure is nice to have someone to talk with,* she thought. Both stood up and took their dishes to the dishwasher. Annalisa hugged her aunt, feeling grateful for her presence.

"Thanks again for being here with me, Aunt Catherine."

"You're welcome, Dear. If I were home alone in that big Sioux City, I'd be having a harder time with my own grief. It sure helps to have someone close to talk with."

Catherine looked down thoughtfully, then looked at Annalisa. "But speaking of the city, I need to go soon to get my things. I only brought enough for two weeks, which has now been three. Since I will be living here, I need to go get the rest of my possessions."

"Will you need to get furniture and everything?"

"My apartment was furnished, so none of the furniture was mine, except my cedar chest. I think I could pack everything into a pickup or small U-Haul trailer. How about if we go tomorrow, and do some cleaning and packing, stay overnight and go to church there?

"That sounds good," Annalisa said. "I usually like our church services, but when I feel so emotional, I'd almost rather be somewhere else. I've already been hugged so much it seems awkward to see the same people again right away."

"We'll do that then. Also, I think it might be too hard on you to go right back to school. How about if we pick up some homework on Monday and you stay out another week?"

"That would be a relief. I'm afraid I would keep bursting out in tears. Thanks Auntie."

Closing Out Aunt Catherine's Apartment

Saturday morning Annalisa noticed the sun was already high in the sky when she opened her eyes. "Aunt Catherine, why didn't you wake me? I thought you wanted to go to Sioux City?"

"There's still plenty of time. I wanted to make sure you slept as long as you could, since I heard you up in the night. Did you have trouble sleeping again?"

"Yes, I kept having dumb dreams." Annalisa turned back to the bedroom to get dressed.

When Annalisa came back to the kitchen, she asked, "Have you contacted your boss?"

"Yes, I called him on Monday and told him I had to resign, effective immediately. He said he would give me a good reference and severance pay, since I've been a good employee for six years."

"Since college?"

"No, I worked at another place for four years."

"Will you hate to leave there?"

"No, not really. It was a good job for paying bills, but it wasn't a fulfillment of a dream or anything like that. And the only co-employee who was really a friend left for her dream job a couple months ago. I do miss her, but we keep in touch by mail."

"Mail is nice."

After a pleasant drive, they stopped at her apartment along a quiet street. They packed and cleaned for the rest of the day, taking breaks only for lunch and supper. Annalisa packed books while Catherine packed her clothes, filling three suitcases. Then they started on the kitchen. "I wish we had a pickup and a couple strong men to help us," Catherine said. "Maybe at church tomorrow someone will offer to help. Or, if we rent a U-Haul trailer, maybe someone there could help us load up."

"We should have asked Todd and Travis to come along," Annalisa said. "But I think they had football today. But if we can get a U-Haul loaded, I think they would help us unload it."

The next day, they went to the church Catherine had been attending.

Annalisa felt relieved to be going to church in Sioux City instead of at home. Usually, she loved her church. But right now, she felt too emotionally drained to go there. She had enjoyed visiting Catherine's church before, and looked forward to being there again. Catherine seemed to be well-loved and many people expressed their sympathy to her over the death of her brother and sister-in-law. Catherine introduced her to a couple of her best friends, but didn't overload her with too many introductions.

One awkward moment came when an acquaintance asked, "And who is this lovely young lady?" Catherine answered that she was her niece and the lady said, "Oh, you mean your brother's daughter? Oh, my, then she's an orphan now!" Annalisa cringed at the painful word, yet tried to be pleasant to the lady. Feeling a difficulty in breathing, she asked her aunt to excuse her and bolted for the door to get some fresh air.

Later Catherine apologized for her acquaintance. "She is so outspoken, but she is actually a sweet lady. She just doesn't realize how she sounds sometimes."

They had lunch at a cozy family-style restaurant. The atmosphere seemed to calm Annalisa's stirred-up emotions. By dessert time, she could chuckle when Catherine recited a joke the minister had included in his sermon.

"Oh, by the way," Catherine said as they finished dessert, "My friend's husband offered to bring a friend and come help us load the U-Haul Trailer later this afternoon, so we will go pick it up now. We have the heaviest boxes packed, and the cedar chest and suitcases are ready. After they load those, we can load the rest later. We won't finish cleaning today. I can do that when I bring the U-Haul back."

"Where will you put your cedar chest, Aunt Catherine?" Annalisa asked on the way.

"I measured the space at the foot of the guest room bed, where I sleep. I think it will fit there, although a little crowded. I hope Todd and Travis can carry it in from the U-Haul trailer. It is too heavy for you and I."

"They seemed sincere about wanting to help when they could. I will call them when we get home. I'll tell them I need a couple strong big brothers."

By the time they picked up the trailer and arrived back at the apartment, the two men arrived to help. It didn't take long for them to load the cedar chest and heavy boxes and the suitcases. Catherine and Annalisa thanked them and tried to pay them, but they refused any money. "We were just glad to help you out," they said.

After they added a few small things and were on the way back to Gardenia, Annalisa was curious. "Aunt Catherine?"

"Yes?"

"What is in your cedar chest? You seem to be very fond of it."

"I am fond of it. My big brother made it for me." She smiled at the memory.

"My Dad? Really? It is a work of art!" She had another sharp pang of missing her dad.

"Yes, it is. He was eighteen years old and taking shop as a senior in high school. My birthday was in May and I would be thirteen years old. He decided every teenage girl should have a hope chest, so he made one for me in shop class. The inside is lined with real cedar, which smells wonderful and also keeps moths away."

"So what did you put in it?"

"Every Christmas after that, he would give me things he thought I might like to have when I got married: pillowcases with pretty embroidery, tablecloths, knick knacks, bath towels, Christmas tree ornaments. Sometimes our parents would give something for it, but usually they gave me clothes or other more immediate needs. After Bob got married, Marcia helped him choose a beautiful nightgown for me. I also keep my diary in there. That is why it's locked." She smiled.

"Oh," said Annalisa, "you'll have to read it to me."

"Probably not."

"Did you ever get close to being married?"

"Sort of close. At least, I was in love once." Catherine turned a lovely shade of pink. "It is a long story. I'll tell you some other time."

By the time they arrived at home they were exhausted, so went right to bed.

The next day, Catherine and Annalisa went to the school to talk with the guidance counselor, Mrs. Hoffman.

"Hello, Miss Schuiteman, hello Annalisa. I heard what happened and I'm so sorry!" She invited them to sit down on a couch in her room.

"Thank you," Annalisa said. She looked at Catherine, waiting for her to speak.

"We are wondering if there will be any problem with Annalisa catching up on her schoolwork if she stays out another week. When I called last Monday after I heard the news, and said she wouldn't be here for a few days, the secretary said not to worry about it but to come talk to you when she felt ready to return."

"How do you feel about returning, Annalisa?"

"Well, I still have bad dreams and wake up screaming and crying, and then I'm so tired the next day. Also, I'm afraid I'll burst out in tears during class."

"Yes," said Mrs. Hoffman, "it sounds like you need a little more time to adjust. That's certainly understandable. Let's plan on you taking another week off, then check in with me when you return. I'm sure your teachers will understand and will help you the best they can. I'll send out messages requesting homework and you may pick that up later today."

Catherine nodded and thanked her.

"The reason I've asked the secretary to send you to me," she continued, "is so I can advise you of some helps. For one thing, we do have a grief support group here at the school which meets during the noon hour each Tuesday. It is led by Travis Klein and there are several students who attend. Many of them lost a parent or sibling years ago, a few more recently. Have you heard about it, Annalisa?"

"Yes, Travis told me about it."

"They talk about their feelings, and Travis has had some training which prepares him in leading the discussion. So that's one thing you could try and see if it helps you adjust to your loss. Another thing I want to tell you is that if you seem to be stuck in one of the stages of grief, for instance if you not only feel sad, which is normal, but you feel depressed to the point of not being able to cope with things, you may come and see me. I will visit with you, and if we decide professional counseling would help, I'll refer you to a professional counselor. If you don't have insurance to cover it, the school's insurance will pay for it."

"Thank you, Mrs. Hoffman. That is reassuring," Catherine said. "I had worried about how to help Annalisa if she became depressed."

"You are welcome," Mrs. Hoffman said. "There is also an adult Grief Share group that meets in the library basement each Thursday noon."

"Now, about your schoolwork, Annalisa; since you are an excellent student, I don't think you'll have much trouble catching up if you miss these two weeks. Each teacher will give you a list of your necessary make-up assignments. They will give you an extra week or more before assignments are due. I would suggest you do the current assignments first (unless they need to be in sequence) and then as much of the catch up work as you can each day. Do you have any questions?"

"No, I think you've explained it all well. Did you say it is okay to come talk with you if I have any problems in school?" Annalisa asked.

"Yes, it is definitely okay. Is there something you have in mind?"

"Well, there is a girl who seems not to like me, and sometimes she says things that hurt."

"Oh dear." Mrs. Hoffman frowned. "Unfortunately that is far too common. Of course, you may come and talk with me any time. Come during your study hall or noon hour or before or after school. Just make an appointment with my secretary and she will give you a pass. Or, if it's an emergency, just come right in and tell my secretary. If I'm busy, you can wait or I can call you out of class. One thing that might help is to remember that people who act like that are usually hurting inside themselves, and they don't know how to handle it. So they take it out on people who, they think, have things in life better than they do. If you can act with compassion and try to be friendly, perhaps she will change."

"Thank you. I'll try."

After leaving the school, the two mourners brought into their house what they could of Catherine's things and found places for them. Then they took a nap. Late that afternoon, Annalisa called Todd. "We need a couple strong men to carry Aunt Catherine's cedar chest and some heavy boxes into the house. Would you be willing and able to do that?"

"Sure. I'll talk to Travis and then call you back about the time."

Annalisa smiled slightly to herself as she put her smart phone back into her pocket. *He sure has a nice voice. And he sounded so glad to help.*

Annalisa was glad when Catherine invited the guys to stay for supper after they had done the job. At first, when they all sat down at the dining room table, they sat stiff and proper. *Why do they want to be friends with me?* Annalisa wondered. *Are they trustworthy?*

Travis cleared his throat. "Todd and I have each lost a parent, so we know what it might feel like. We are in that grief support group I mentioned to you, which gives some teaching about how to get safely through grief. Regular attendance at the youth group has also been a great help both in fellowship and in teaching us how to follow Jesus Christ. It has stimulated us to want to serve our Lord Jesus by reaching out to others who are grieving like we have grieved. We just want to be friends to both of you.

Annalisa could see her aunt visibly relax. "That's very thoughtful and kind of you. I am relieved, because I wondered if you wanted to date Annalisa. She is too young to date."

Todd glanced at Annalisa. "Travis and I realize that. She is very pretty, and there may be some boys who would try to take advantage of her vulnerability and loneliness to persuade her to do things she shouldn't do. We would like to be like big brothers to her for protection and help in whatever ways we can. Sticking together as we do, we also keep each other accountable to do the right thing." He looked at Travis, who smiled and nodded.

Annalisa relaxed. *I think I can trust these guys. It sure is nice of them to want to help.*

"Eat up, boys," said Catherine. "I hope you like cookies for dessert. We just baked some."

Among other things, they talked about the homecoming game coming up in less than a month, on October 22nd. "We should be able to win this time," Travis said.

Todd looked at Annalisa with a hopeful expression. "Will you come and watch the game?" he asked.

"I think so—I'm not sure." Annalisa felt a little uncertain about getting into the spirit of the game. She suddenly felt an enormous heaviness. Her dad used to like football. Sometimes both parents used to go with her to a game.

Soon after the boys left, Annalisa said goodnight to her aunt and went to her room. She cried herself to sleep again and had another bad dream. Her dad was at a football game with her, then all of a sudden he was in an airplane over the field and the airplane crashed right on the football field on top of the players. She woke up screaming and then dissolved in tears. Her aunt came and lay beside her for awhile.

Tuesday they slept late; then they took the U-Haul trailer back to Sioux City, finished cleaning the apartment, and packed up the remaining odds and ends to take home.

It seemed to Annalisa that the week went by in a painful blur. She tried to do homework, but could concentrate only a few minutes at a time. However, by Friday she was finally making some progress on it.

Annalisa and Catherine also did some much needed cleaning and baking on Friday. "It feels invigorating to keep physically busy after the emotional exhaustion of the past two weeks," her aunt said, and Annalisa agreed.

On Saturday afternoon, as they had planned, Travis and Todd came over. *Yes, they really did "bring a little sunshine,"* Annalisa thought, although her heart still felt like lead. They played games and Todd shared jokes from a joke book.

"Are you going back to school Monday?" Travis asked, when they got up to leave.

"Yes. I've been out two weeks already, and it will be hard enough to catch up," Annalisa said. "Besides, if I stay home, I'll just miss my parents more."

"We can give you rides to school, since we live only a block away from you. It may be chilly in the mornings, but shouldn't be too bad in the afternoons for a while yet."

Catherine answered, "I will take her to school this Monday, since I want to talk with the guidance counselor. After that, you may give her rides if you wish and she agrees."

Todd said, "We both have football practice after school until 4:30 or 5 for about four more weeks. After that, we could give you a ride both ways."

"I'll dress warm," said Annalisa. "I don't mind walking home until then."

Travis said, "We missed you at youth group this week, but of course we all understood. Would you like us to pick you up for Youth Group this Wednesday evening?"

"Yes, that would be nice. Thank you."

Annalisa started to say something else, then thought, *am I ready for this? Will it help, or just remind me how much I miss my parents?* She took a deep breath, then said, "I think it will be good for me to go to that grief support group on Tuesday. Maybe it will help to talk to others my age who have some idea what grief feels like."

"Great," said Travis. "We'll be glad to have you. We meet in that room off the library."

Annalisa nodded. *But I am sort of scared to go back to school Monday. If anything goes wrong, I'm not sure I could handle it,* she thought. She felt her chest tighten up.

Sunday, sitting by Catherine, she felt kind of numb through the first half of the worship service, although the hymns were somewhat comforting, bringing tears to her eyes. Catherine took her hand in hers and gently squeezed it. Annalisa noticed tears in her aunt's eyes, also.

The church had provided a prayer blanket for Annalisa, and during the service they had a time set for people to tie the fringe, indicating they would be praying for her. They gave it to her after the service. They had done this for the others the week before.

What a sweet thing to do, Annalisa thought. *Again she had the sensation of God spreading a blanket of peace over her.*

Brenda's Return to School

*M*onday morning Brenda prepared to resume her school schedule, after missing for two weeks. *I still feel weak,* she thought. *I'd never felt so sick before.* The walk was tiring, so she sat down on a bench near the school to rest. *I'm glad I started early.*

Soon she saw Annalisa and a woman get out of a car. *I wonder who that is with Annalisa. She usually walks to school.* When Brenda gave her doctor's note to the school secretary at the office, she saw Annalisa receive a back-to-class permit also. *I wonder why she's been absent?*

But she didn't have time to find out now. She had to talk to her math teacher before school started. There was a math problem she didn't understand. Then it was time to get to English class. The teacher smiled as the bell rang. "It's good to see both Annalisa and Brenda back," she said. "We have missed you."

Brenda exchanged a puzzled glance with Annalisa. *Why was she absent?* she wondered.

Brenda hung back after class, hoping maybe she could talk with Annalisa, but she wasn't surprised that Annalisa didn't even look her way. *I wonder if she got hurt badly when I ran into her two weeks ago.* She tried to push the thought out of her mind.

The next two classes went quickly, then it was lunchtime. Brenda hurried to the lunchroom so she could take her lunch to Mrs. Hoffman's room and eat with her. She saw Annalisa sitting by Todd and Travis. *Boy, she sure is lucky,* Brenda thought. *She not only has lots of girl friends but also handsome boyfriends. I wish I could be popular like her.*

Brenda picked up her lunch, then turned around and saw Annalisa nearby putting her tray on the conveyor belt.

"Well, if it isn't the Princess, looking so spiffy, and now flirting with upperclassmen. Where have you been for the past two weeks?"

"Hello, Brenda." Annalisa turned to walk away, but Brenda blocked her path.

"Cat got your tongue? I said where have you been?"

Annalisa sighed. She spoke softly. "I've been planning and attending the Home-going service of my parents," she said crisply, without looking at Brenda.

Brenda was surprised. "What's a Home-going service?"

"It's like a funeral. They got killed in an airplane crash."

Oh no! That's terrible! Why can't I say something comforting? Brenda thought, standing there like a stone. Finally, she said in a shocked voice, "So now, you're an orphan!" and stared at Annalisa, blankly. *Here I was jealous of her family, and now she's alone!*

Annalisa clenched her fists, then walked away stiffly while Brenda watched.

Todd and Travis caught up to Annalisa and walked out with her.

Brenda walked to Mrs. Hoffman's office, feeling rather shaky.

"Hello Brenda. You may sit here. I've brought my lunch from home today. And how does it feel to be back to school?"

"The morning went fairly well, but I feel kind of sick now."

"Oh? In what way?" Mrs. Hoffman had a look Brenda had never seen in a teacher before, a look of tenderness and concern, like she really cared. Maybe for a change she could really share her feelings with an adult and get some advice that would help. She took a bite of her mashed potatoes. Mrs. Hoffman waited.

Brenda put down her spoon and looked up. "Well, I've been having these jealous feelings about this girl, and now I just found out her parents got killed. I feel all stirred-up inside."

"You feel conflicting emotions?" Mrs. Hoffman asked. Somehow Brenda felt she understood how she felt.

"Yes. Part of me wants to cry and part of me wants to laugh. Part of me is scared. And a big part of me is so sorry for the way I've been acting toward her."

"Shall we see if we can take each emotion out of the mix and examine it?"

"You mean, like, why do I want to cry?"

"Yes." Mrs. Hoffman gave her an encouraging smile.

"I want to cry because I really like her and wish I could comfort her. She had such nice parents and I know she'll miss them. But I also want to cry because of the way I've been acting toward her. I've been mean because of my jealousy and said things that must have hurt her. Like, the Friday before I got sick, we collided in the hall. I didn't mean to bump into her, but when it happened I was glad I knocked her down and made her drop all her stuff because I was so jealous and angry."

"Jealousy is a terrible emotion. It often hurts more people than the person who indulges in it. You say another part of you wants to laugh? Why?"

Brenda picked at her food. She didn't want to admit this part because she was ashamed of it. "I guess I still feel jealous. At least she had parents who loved her, and who cared about her interests and encouraged her in them. And she's pretty, and sweet, and popular, and dresses nicely and everybody likes her." By this time Brenda was weeping, quietly.

Mrs. Hoffman came around the desk to sit by her and hold her hand. "It's understandable that you would want those things. It's hard to understand why life is the way it is."

Too soon, the warning bell rang. It was time to get to class.

"Would you like to talk again next Monday? Or would you like me to refer you to a more professional counselor who can help you with these deep emotions?"

Brenda jumped a little. "Oh no! I don't want to talk to anyone else. You're the only one I really feel comfortable with. Besides, my mother wouldn't let me take time to do anything else outside of school. But do I have to wait until Monday?"

"Lunchtime works quite well. You may come again on Thursday if you wish."

"Thank you. That'd be great. Bye now." Mrs. Hoffman smiled and Brenda hurried out the door.

Orphan!

That same Monday morning, Annalisa woke early and dressed in her favorite school outfit which was a red and black pleated skirt, with a white blouse over which she wore a red crew neck sweater. Her black flats completed the outfit. She shouldered her backpack and headed down the stairs to the deliciously appealing odor of bacon, scrambled eggs and toast.

"Oh, Aunt Catherine, this smells so good."

"Well, I figured you needed a good breakfast to start your day on your first day back to school. You look very nice in that outfit and with your pretty blonde hair."

"Thank you." When she'd finished eating and had brushed her teeth, Annalisa put her backpack in the car. Catherine drove her to school early in case there would be any problems. They checked in with Mrs. Hoffman, who asked, "How are you coping with your grief?"

Annalisa thought a moment, then answered, "At least by the end of the week I could concentrate a little better on homework. I still feel really sad and sometimes have nightmares."

"Have you considered attending the grief support group tomorrow?"

"Yes, I think that would be helpful."

"Good. I'm sure what you are feeling is normal after such a loss. But if you don't start feeling better in a couple weeks and want to talk to a professional counselor, let me know.

"Yes, I will."

Annalisa felt glad she could get through the morning without crying, although she still missed her parents so much. *Praying for God's grace to be sufficient must have helped,* she thought. *I'll need to keep praying for grace sufficient. It will take a lot of time and effort to catch up on past homework while doing the current homework.*

At lunchtime, she met up with Mary Lou in the hall. They saw Todd and Travis eating together and sat down beside them. "Hi guys. Thanks again for helping us last week."

"Hi Annalisa," they both said. "Hi Mary Lou."

"Those delicious cookies with supper made it worth it," Todd said with a grin.

Annalisa smiled. "I'm glad you liked them. I'll bake a double batch for you sometime." For a moment, she felt happy, seeing his sunny smile.

When Annalisa took her dishes to the conveyor belt, she heard a familiar, dreaded voice.

"Well, if it isn't the Princess, looking so spiffy, and now flirting with upperclassmen. Where have you been for the past two weeks?"

"Hello, Brenda." She tried to just walk away, but Brenda blocked her path.

"Cat got your tongue? I said where have you been?"

Annalisa sighed. She didn't need this harassment. "I've been planning and attending the Home-going service of my parents," she said crisply, without looking at Brenda.

Brenda sounded surprised. "What's a Homegoing service?"

"It's like a funeral. They got killed in an airplane crash." For a moment Annalisa thought Brenda might express her sympathy.

Instead, Brenda said in a shocked voice, "So now, you're an orphan!" staring at her.

Annalisa clenched her fists, then walked away while tears filled her eyes and spilled over.

Todd and Travis and Mary Lou caught up to her and walked her to class. "We heard what she said," said Travis. She just doesn't know how to be friendly."

"You did good in answering her and then walking away," said Todd. "Most people would have said something unkind in turn." She felt grateful for their concern and their presence, but oh, how her heart hurt! Why did God allow her to hurt so much?

Somehow, she made it through the afternoon.

When Annalisa got home that afternoon, the house smelled good. "What are you baking, Aunt Catherine?"

"Banana bread. It is cooling. Soon you may have a piece."

"Good." She put her backpack on the stairs to take up later, and sat down at the table.

"Remember that girl I told you about? The one that says things to hurt me?"

"Yes. Did she do it again?"

"Yes. She used to call me Smarty Pants. Now she calls me "Orphan." Annalisa's eyes filled with tears again as she remembered.

"Orphan is not necessarily a mean name," said Aunt Catherine. It simply indicates you don't have parents here on earth."

"I know. But it's the way she says it that sounds so mean—like she's trying to rub it in."

"Remember what Mrs. Hoffman said? Maybe she is hurting inside."

"Maybe, but I hate that word. I don't want to be an orphan." Annalisa sobbed.

Catherine came to her and hugged her. "I know. Of course you don't." After a few moments, she said, "You know, you aren't really an orphan—at least you're not an orphan spiritually. God is your father. He has adopted you as his child. He will never leave you nor forsake you. Besides, even though your parents are no longer on this earth, their souls are still alive. Jesus said, "I am the resurrection and the life. He who believes in me will live, even though he dies, and whoever lives and believes in me will never die," (John 11:25-26). I believe your parents are talking to Jesus about you, asking him to provide everything you need."

Annalisa wiped her eyes and smiled at Catherine. She sure was good at helping her feel better. She started on her homework and made good progress before and after supper.

Later that night, she had another nightmare. She woke up feeling her aunt's hands on her arms shaking her gently and hearing her say, "Wake up, Dear, you're having a nightmare. I heard you yelling."

Annalisa sat up and threw herself into her aunt's arms, sobbing. "Brenda was like a monster on all sides of me, just calling me "Orphan, Orphan, Smarty Pants," and other bad names. She spit in my face and pulled my hair. Then she pushed me down a hill."

Catherine hugged her tight and rocked her until she calmed down. Then she gave her a towel to wipe her face. "It sounds a little like persecution—like what they did to Jesus," she commented.

After Catherine went back to bed, Annalisa lay in bed thinking about that. *What was it Jesus said to do to our enemies?* She turned on the light and grabbed her Bible from the bedside stand. Turning to Matthew, she found the Sermon on the Mount. "Blessed are you when [Brenda] reviles and persecutes you... (Mt. 5:11). She read on until she found, "love your enemies, bless those who curse you, do good to those who hate you, and pray for those who spitefully use you and persecute you," (Mt. 5:44). Then she prayed, "Lord, thank you that I can know you. Please help me act in love, especially toward Brenda."

Soon she felt the warm blanket of peace covering her and slept soundly until morning.

12

Grief Support Group

Annalisa put up her hood to shield from the brisk wind. "Thanks for the ride, guys," she said to Todd and Travis. "I'll see you at the group meeting at noon." She ran quickly into the school. Brenda stopped her in the hall and said, "Hello, Orphan."

Annalisa tried not to let her see that the name hurt her, but instead smiled as sweetly as she could muster. "Hello, Brenda. God bless you." Then, she hurried away. She didn't see Brenda again the rest of the day.

At noon Annalisa picked up her sack lunch from her locker and hurried to the Grief Support Group meeting in the library. She felt shy going in, but Todd welcomed her and led her to a chair. She saw several students she knew and soon was more concerned about their grief than her shyness. Mrs. Hoffman was there, and so was a man she didn't recognize. He looked too old to be a student, yet still quite young.

Travis was apparently the moderator. He welcomed everyone and explained the rules of the group. "What is said here is for your ears alone. Please do not tell anyone else. We give each person a chance to speak if they want to, and others can respond with encouraging and supportive short comments. But please, no judging of feelings. We don't tell each other 'You shouldn't feel that way.' Feelings are neither right nor wrong. They just are, and each person should feel free to express them."

Mrs. Hoffman stood up "We have two new members of our group today. Ricardo De La Vega lost his grandparents and Annalisa Schuiteman lost her parents, both in the same accident. The plane they and 18 others were on crashed on its way home from a mission trip to Ecuador. Please make Ricardo and Annalisa feel welcome."

A few students got up quietly and either shook hands or patted a shoulder or just said hi to the two new ones. Annalisa warmed to their sincerity. She was grateful that it didn't seem like a stiff, formal group.

Travis looked around the group. When all were seated again, he said, "For our first time around the circle, would each of you tell your name and tell how long it has been since your loved one died?"

Mrs. Hoffman stood up. "First, Travis, may I introduce this young man?"

Travis nodded.

"This is Jeff Leeds. He is the new youth Pastor at Trinity Lutheran here in Gardenia. He has also had special training in Grief counseling, similar to what Travis has had, but more extensive. Therefore, he has insights that may help us."

Pastor Leeds stood up and said, "Hello. I am also a mourner like you, having lost my wife and baby three years ago, shortly after I was ordained. That is why I went through the extensive training—to look for help and answers. My purpose here is the same as yours—to share each others' journeys and share what has been helpful to me in my grief. One thing most helpful to me was being allowed to cry. I had the impression growing up that 'men don't cry' so at first I didn't know what to do with the terrible ache inside of me. Then one day my Pastor came to me and said it's okay to cry. He was so sympathetic that I was able to tell him about my feelings, and then he actually cried with me. It was such a relief."

As they spoke around the circle, Annalisa noticed that there were students from each of the four grades of high school. Their loved ones had died anywhere from two weeks ago to many years ago. She was surprised at how many there were.

When everyone else had spoken Travis said, "My name, as you know, is Travis Klein and my loss was eight years ago. Now let's go around the circle again and give each person a chance to tell of something that has helped you so far. Or you can share your feelings."

Annalisa listened with interest as one after the other spoke. She realized they were going through basically the same experience she was. Although the details were different, the feelings were much the same. Tears flowed freely and no one seemed to mind. It impressed her that everyone seemed so supportive of each other. Although she still felt almost like a stranger, she was glad she came.

Todd spoke after several others. "One thing important to remember is that each one's grief is unique. People process things differently, so one should not tell another what to feel."

Then it was Annalisa's turn. "My grief is still quite new. I have nightmares at night, and I feel awfully tired during the day. I never know when I might burst into tears. I often feel such a pain in my chest, I think there must be a hole there."

A few people nodded. "You sound normal. Some of us have said in previous meetings that we experienced the same things," a classmate named Julie said. Annalisa felt grateful to her.

"What do you do about these feelings then?" Annalisa asked.

"Some of us have had counseling for our nightmares. It helped me, I know. Some of this stuff you just have to wade through until enough time passes that your emotions begin healing."

Later as they were getting ready to leave, Julie came up to her and said, "Hugs help, too." Then she gave Annalisa a big bear hug.

As Annalisa went to the next class, she thought of the things "the mourners" had said. It was encouraging and she looked forward to the next meetings.

After school, Annalisa planned to walk home, but was glad to see her aunt coming to pick her up. "Nice surprise, Aunt Catherine," she said, getting into the car.

"I had gone to the store for something, so thought I might as well swing by."

Annalisa thought there was something hidden in Catherine's smile when she asked, "Did you feel the grief support meeting was worthwhile?"

"Yes, I did. I'm glad I went. I never realized so many in our school had lost loved ones. Some of them were grandparents, which is more understandable because they're old. But some had lost a sister or brother, or a parent. One lost her parents and two sisters all at once in a car accident. Most of these had died many years ago, but were still grieving. Travis started this group last spring, with Mrs. Hoffman's help, and I think it's really a good idea."

"Has he lost a family member?"

By this time they had reached the house, so Annalisa got out of the car before answering.

"Yes, eight years ago his mother died of cancer."

"Oh my, so he was quite young."

"Yes, only ten years old. He had a rough time of it."

As they entered the house, Aunt Catherine said, "Annalisa, you received a letter today."

13

The Letter

Annalisa looked at her aunt. "A letter?" Why did her aunt sound so strange? She saw tears in her eyes, then was engulfed in a bear hug. Her aunt held her tightly for a long moment, then released her and handed her the letter. It had a strange postmark. *Ecuador! That's my Mom's handwriting!* First a feeling of joy filled her heart. *Then they're not dead, after all!*

Then she felt confused. She looked at Aunt Catherine. The look on her face reminded her of Pastor Brady's news. No, there was no doubt they'd been killed. She went into the living room and sank into a comfortable chair, then opened the letter and noticed the date: September 8th. Almost a month ago. Tears flowed as she began. She had to keep wiping them away in order to see to read.

Dear Annalisa,   Sept. 8

We've been here a week now and we miss you so much. The Lord is obviously working through the whole team in mighty ways, so we are glad we came. Yet, we miss you, our dear, beloved daughter and we hope things are going well with you.

As you said, things are very primitive here. After our arrival in Ecuador, we rode on a bus up narrow mountain roads wide enough for one vehicle. Ruts in the road sometimes caused our vehicle to lean so far to one side, I was afraid we'd tip over. About an hour into the journey, the driver stopped the bus and backed up, slowly. When he reached a wider spot in the road, he pulled as close to the mountain side as possible and stopped. Soon another bus came around the corner, traveling down the mountain. As it passed, the drivers waved to each other. The canyon floor is a long way down the mountain side, so it was scary. We felt relieved to reach the village, in spite of its primitive nature. The team members jest a lot, which makes it fun and helps take our minds off the scary ride and primitive conditions.

Annalisa paused in her reading. *I remember when I tried to talk them into not going. Mom said, "That is exactly why we are going, to help improve conditions so they'll have a better life. We'll also tell them about Jesus, and maybe a few of the people will accept Him as Savior."* She nodded to herself and continued reading.

With all of us pitching in, it didn't take long to put up the tents. I'm assigned to help teach the women about hygiene, safe food handling, baby care, and treatments for minor illnesses. Your Dad is the construction foreman.

The people live in shacks that don't even keep out the rain and cold. They not only don't have indoor toilets, they don't even have decent outhouses. Rather, they didn't before we came. That is one of the first things the men did— build latrines and teach them how to use them. Then they taught better farming practices to conserve soil and produce more crops. Some of the farmers here still use the same techniques their great-grandfathers used. Next week they plan to build a chapel.

The first morning, after only a few hours of sleep, they woke your Dad to deal with a problem. Several tools and construction materials were missing. They went to see the village Chief who, fortunately, spoke and understood English.

"Sir," Bob said, "Some of our tools and materials are missing. Will you help us find the things on this list?"

"Will help," said Chief in broken English. "Follow me." Soon they saw the materials behind a hut. A man appeared in the doorway of the hut. The Chief spoke to him in their dialect. He answered back, then the Chief told our men to pick them up. He turned to the thief and motioned for him to follow. He obediently walked behind the Chief, head down.

Our fellows wondered what would happen to the thief. A couple of them followed to find out. The Chief led the thief to the edge of the village where he bound the thief's hands and feet and then bound him to a tree.

"Wife come feed him four days, then I free him," he told our men. "He not steal from you again. No one else steal from you." Chief struck his fist against his chest, as if making a promise.

Our men worked hard all week, digging pits and constructing buildings over them for latrines. They also showed the village men how to line their fire pits with cement blocks, and they built washing stations. When these were all done, they told the Chief to instruct his people to be sure to wash their hands after using the latrines. Much of the disease problems in their village come because people relieve themselves behind trees or bushes and then others come in contact with the waste material. If they have open sores on their feet, germs, parasites, and worms can get in and cause them to become ill.

"We will make villagers use latrines and wash," said the Chief, with a frown that defied anyone to go against his bidding.

Then Bob gave him shovels and told him "When a latrine is full, cover the pit with dirt—at least this much dirt." He demonstrated by holding his hands twelve inches apart. "Your village will be healthier and happier if you follow our suggestions."

Meanwhile, we gathered the village ladies and teenage girls in the center of the village. We tried to gain their trust first by building relationships, telling about ourselves and asking about their families. It's difficult to communicate, even though we'd all studied the language some, but a few were able to translate, so we managed. Praise the Lord for answered prayers.

About the third day, we taught intensive health classes. We had learned through conversations that most of them have frequent illness in the family—many stomach problems, headaches, diarrhea. We tested their water and found it to be contaminated. There's no other source of water except for the lake, so we taught them always to boil their drinking and cooking water, as well as to wash and cook their food.

Some were offended. "We would not give our children food or water that is bad," they said. I assured them we know they wouldn't do that on purpose. But I showed them samples of the water and food (both before and after boiling or cooking) under the microscope we had brought along. Then they could see what I was talking about.

We taught the villagers about dehydration from diarrhea and the re-hydration solution. (This information could come in handy for you sometime when you have children. We mix six level teaspoons of sugar with ½ level teaspoon of salt and one liter of clean drinking water or boiled water.) We brought bottles of Pedialyte along which is a flavored version of the same thing. Then we give sips, or a teaspoon, of either solution every few minutes until the diarrhea stops. We have begun giving it to several babies who appear dehydrated.

In the evenings after supper, the members of our mission team meet together for devotions and for comparing experiences. We all are pleased with the response of the villagers, and feel God is working through us for their good.

After treating many with the re-hydration solution, I took out a large bottle of deworming medicine and told them it would help their children stop being sick. Suddenly, the village "doctor" watching the scene announced, "Medicine not work here! Works only in United States." I challenged the village "doctor" to a contest. I would treat ten villagers with this medicine, and he would treat ten others his way. After a week they would compare the twenty subjects. "The ones I treat will sleep in a tent next to my tent," I said. "Doctor, your ten can stay at home. Yes?"

Reluctantly, the doctor said "Yes." Several women begged to be on my side. A few more skeptical women sided with the village doctor. If the patient who tries the medicine is a young child, the mother will stay in the tent by me, also. Next Thursday, we will determine which group is healthier.

Goodbye for now, Annalisa. We will try to send this letter down the mountain tomorrow so you can receive it before we return. God bless you and keep you safe. We love you very much.

Love Mom and Dad.

P.S. September 17. I'm sorry, Annalisa, but there was no one to take the letter to the post office. I'm going to add some and mail it before we get on the plane tomorrow. I suppose we could just as well take it to you ourselves, but I think it will be exciting for you to receive a letter from a foreign country.

We continued to instruct and befriend the ladies, while the contest continued. Having some in the nearby tent gave us opportunities to minister the gospel to them. Today the village "doctor" examined each of the patients, his and ours, then sheepishly declared to the chief, "Her patients get well, mine don't." So, he's willing to use the medicine we leave. We will leave several bottles of Pedialite and antibiotics, also.

You're going to think this is funny, Annalisa. I know you told your Dad you hoped he would lose his silly-looking hat. He did. It flew off his head in a wind one day, and disappeared in the jungle. He laughed about it and said, "Well, I guess that's a sign my little Princess is praying for me!"

Today the Chief said goodbye to the group because he will be gone tomorrow when we leave. He shook everyone's hand and hugged the men. "Our village thankful for your work and how you treat us," he said.

We are glad we came, too. May the Lord use it for his glory.

Love, Mom and Dad.

Annalisa sat quietly for a long moment after reading the letter. Her face was wet with tears, but somehow the letter helped. Her heart didn't hurt quite as bad. She smiled about the hat, remembering how she'd teased her dad about that. She remembered asking him why he always called her Princess. He'd replied, "It's because when I first saw you, after your birth, I felt like a King. So I called you my Princess. I'm so very proud of you. You've been a wonderful daughter. I know some day you'll meet a young man and want to be married. Please be sure he is a Christian who serves God."

I will Daddy. Thank you for making me feel like a Princess.

And Mom—you said you always loved to hear me laugh, that you want me always to be happy because you love me so much. I'm so blessed to have had parents like you two.

Annalisa went to the kitchen to find her aunt. "Aunt Catherine," she said, "Thanks for giving me privacy to read it. You may read it now." She handed her the letter and went upstairs.

Annalisa's Nightmare

"Let them go! Let them go!" The scream pierced the darkness in the middle of the night. Annalisa heard herself screaming in the jungle. Then she felt gentle hands on her shoulders.

"Annalisa, wake up, you're having a nightmare." Slowly, Annalisa opened her eyes. She looked around confused. Then she recognized Aunt Catherine. She threw herself into her arms, sobbing. As soon as she could speak, she said, "I dreamed I was in Ecuador with my parents and this huge boa constrictor caught me ... then it caught my parents, … it killed my Mom and Dad. It seemed so real! I ran into the jungle and got lost. Things were chasing me. I fell down..."

Aunt Catherine held the trembling girl. "Honey, you've had a terrible experience losing your parents. Here, let me dry these tears from your cheeks." She wiped them with something soft. "I, also, wish your parents had not died, but remember they are now with Jesus. All their troubles and pain are gone. I'm here with you and I'll stay with you."

"Thank you, Auntie." She snuggled against her like a little child.

"Honey, has this nightmare occurred on other nights?"

"Yes, in various forms, but this was the worst."

"Annalisa, I believe you should go to your school counselor and tell her about your dream. Try to go back to sleep now and see your school counselor sometime tomorrow."

"But, what if I have the same dream again tonight?"

"Would you like me to stay in your room for the rest of the night?"

"Yes, please do."

Aunt Catherine crawled into bed with Annalisa and wrapped her arms around her until they both fell asleep. The night passed with no more dreams and both felt better in the morning when the alarm clock rang to wake them.

After breakfast, Annalisa said, "Good bye, Aunt Catherine. I'll stop and see the counselor today." She made an appointment for during her study hall. When the time came, Annalisa felt a little bit nervous. She had not thought she needed a counselor before and she remembered some negative comments made by other students about those who needed counseling. She held her head up and reasoned: *very few students have lost one or both parents, and so they have no idea what such an experience can do to a young girl.*

"Hello, Annalisa, I'm happy to see you," said Mrs. Hoffman. "How may I help you?"

"As you know my parents died in an airplane accident two and a half weeks ago. I've had re-occurring dreams and nightmares about their deaths. I hope you can help me get past those awful dreams."

"Would you like to tell me about the dream, Annalisa?"

"In my dream, I went to Ecuador with my parents and one day we went into the jungle and a boa constrictor wrapped itself around me. I managed to escape its coils, but the snake then captured my parents and took them into the branches of a tall tree. I yelled "Let them go, let them go," which is what Aunt Catherine heard me yelling last night. Once high in the tree, the snake dropped my parents and they died when they struck the jungle floor. I screamed, cried and ran away but became mixed-up and could not find my way out of the jungle, and it was scary."

"Annalisa, I am so sorry for the loss of your parents and that you are now experiencing these nightmares. I wish I could help you, but in this case I think it is better to refer you to a professional counselor at Hope For Life services. Their office is downtown at the corner of Broadway and Main. Are you able to wait while I call them to arrange an appointment for you?"

"Yes, I have time to wait."

The counselor picked up the phone and said, "Hello, yes, this is Mrs. Hoffman at the high school. I have a girl here in my office suffering from the loss of her parents in an airplane crash last month. She is still experiencing nightmares related to the accident. I would like to schedule an appointment for her. She paused, listening.

"Tomorrow after school at 3:30? Thank you. I hope you are able to help her."

"I'll make out an appointment card for you, Annalisa. You'll see Margery Heickson tomorrow (Thursday) at 3:30 p. m. at *Hope For Abundant Life Counseling Center*."

"Thank you, Mrs. Hoffman."

Annalisa had planned to go to youth group that evening, but she kept thinking about the dream and about what she should say until she had a bad headache and didn't want to go.

School on the next day passed quickly and Annalisa soon found herself in a large comfortable chair next to Margery Heickson.

"How may I help you Annalisa?" asked Margery Heickson.

"I don't know what to call you--- Miss, Mrs., or Counselor Heickson," Annalisa said.

"Call me Margery. Tell about your dream," she said, with a welcoming smile.

"It happens over and over. My parents and I are on a mission trip to Ecuador and one day we go to the jungle. While in the jungle a boa constrictor catches me and wraps its coils around me. It starts to constrict, I scream a lot, and Daddy and Mom come and help me escape. Then it seizes my parents. I scream "Let them go, let them go!" I throw rocks at it and hit it with sticks. I kick at it while I continue to scream. All of that is of no use, because it carries my parents high into a tree. Once up high in the tree, the snake drops my parents and they die when they hit the ground. I turn and run into the jungle to get away from the snake, but then I become lost. I can't find my way out of the jungle. Insects and animals are chasing me and I fall down, tearing my clothes and scratching my arms, legs and face." Annalisa was shaking by the time she finished, and tears smarted her eyes.

Margery leaned forward and patted her shoulder gently. "Can you explain how you are feeling as this happens?"

Annalisa began to cry. "I want to save them, but nothing I do or try has any effect on that snake. I failed in my attempt to save them. I should have saved them!"

"How could you have saved them? That boa constrictor is so much larger and stronger than you are."

"I slipped out of its grip. I should have been able to think of a way to save them," She sobbed.

"Annalisa, it was just a dream, but it reflects how you really feel. You weren't even there. How could you have helped them in that situation?"

"I should have prayed more for them, or I should have kept them from going." Annalisa continued sobbing. "I tried to keep them from going, but they refused to cancel their plans." Margery took Annalisa in her arms and held her until she stopped crying and relaxed.

Handing her a tissue she said, "Here, dry your eyes." She waited for the young girl to compose herself. Then she assured her gently, "It wasn't your fault, Annalisa. They had to make their own decisions based on what they believed God was calling them to do."

"I wish they were still alive," said Annalisa.

"Of course you do, because you love them and you want to be near them. You are grieving because you have lost people very dear to you." They sat quietly for a couple minutes."

"Annalisa, you'll always miss your parents, but in time it won't hurt so much. Then you'll realize that, while you still miss them, you can adjust to them being gone and go on with your life and do great things. Eventually, you will think more about how wonderful it was to have them for fifteen years, rather than feeling so sad that they are gone."

"Do you really think so?" asked Annalisa.

"I think so because I believe you know God loves you and has good plans for your life."

"Yes, I do believe that's true."

"I'm sure you work hard on your school work, and that honors your parents. You will feel better when you do the best you are able to do. If you join an extra-curricular activity such as band, orchestra, school plays, or other things that interest you, that may help you enjoy life more again. It will honor your parents to be the best person you can be. Your parents will be so proud of you when you see them again in heaven."

Annalisa smiled weakly. "I was invited to join band, but I told him I was too busy right now because I've joined the grief support group and am in youth group at church."

"Yes, for right now that sounds like plenty. You don't want to overload yourself, because it can be exhausting to go through grief."

"Yes, I have felt exhausted much of the time. But still I have difficulty sleeping."

Margery nodded in understanding. "Be patient with yourself. It will get better."

"Margery, you sound like you've been through this and understand my heart."

"Yes I have, and I think I do understand. My parents died when I was just a little older than you are. I struggled terribly for some time. But it went better when I learned to cling to Romans 8:28. 'We know that in everything God works for good with those who love him, who are called according to his purpose.'" Margery was silent a moment.

"Do you believe that, Annalisa?"

"I did, I mean I do, but it is so hard now."

"When the time is right, God will make some good come of this loss. While you won't thank God for your parents' deaths, I believe you will thank him eventually for using it for good. If you follow Him and remain faithful, you will find yourself happy once more."

"Thank you for your time and help," said Annalisa, as they both stood up.

"Come and see me next week, Annalisa, so we can see if you are doing better. Oh, and one more suggestion: Thanksgiving is coming up. Try to plan to be with people you like and can have fun with. Holidays are harder for people in grief if they are all alone."

Annalisa left the building feeling some better than she had when she had arrived.

Brenda's Nightmare

renda's emotions continued to conflict long after her conversation with Mrs. Hoffman October 4th. That same afternoon, she had another opportunity to feel jealous when she thought of Annalisa. *She's been out of school two weeks like I have, yet on the first day back she already has her World History map finished. Then the teacher has to hold it up to show the class and rave about how good it is. Mine's only half finished, but I can already see it's not that neat.*

Upon returning home that afternoon, Brenda planned to work hard on homework and catch up quickly. However, her mother had that day off from work and was all excited because the college had agreed to let Brenda do a concert the following spring. She spent a half hour talking about it, and then insisted Brenda practice immediately.

"Mother, I need to do homework. I still have a lot to catch up on from being sick."

"You can do homework later. This is more important. It's too easy to slack off on practice if you don't keep a routine going."

So she practiced. But in her frame of mind, she didn't think it did much good. By the time she finished her required four hours and had supper, she couldn't keep her eyes open long enough to do much homework. So, she was not only not catching up, she was getting further behind. Wednesday, she flunked the spelling quiz in English. *Of course Annalisa got 100% correct.* By the time she got home that afternoon, she was so jealous and angry she couldn't see straight so, again, it was difficult to get much homework done.

Thursday, the one thing that made Brenda want to get out of bed was her appointment with Mrs. Hoffman. However, she received a note during second period that the counselor was sick and wouldn't be able to meet until Monday.

Then there was the nightmare. She'd had this nightmare before, but this time Annalisa was in it. There was chaos and confusion, yelling and doors slamming. She was dressed up to go somewhere with her dad, but she couldn't find him. Then Annalisa found the map of how to find him, but she wouldn't give it to her. By the time Brenda approached school on Friday morning, she felt like Annalisa was her arch enemy.

That's why, when Annalisa came around that hedge, Brenda called her a "spiffy princess" and asked why she was "dressed fit to kill."

The Confrontation

The morning after her meeting with Margery Heickson, Annalisa came around a large hedge on her way to school. She could have had a ride, but it was such a beautiful morning, she had texted Todd and told him she would walk.

She jumped when she heard a voice. "Well, if it isn't the spiffy princess."

Annalisa turned to see a girl staring at her from a nearby bench. *She must have been waiting for me.* Her pulse beat faster as she looked around and saw no one else nearby.

Annalisa tried to sound calm. "Hello, Brenda."

"Hello, *Anal-isa*," she said. "Is this how you 'dress to kill?' Whose dreams are you going to kill today? Or are you just dressed nice so you'll dazzle the teachers into giving you 'A's?'"

"Brenda, why are you so sarcastic to me? Are you sarcastic to everyone?"

"Just you. You think you're so smart 'cuz you're pretty and have such nice clothes, flawless skin, and a thin body," Brenda said. She stuck out her tongue at her.

"I'm sorry you feel jealous, Brenda, but I don't know what to do about it. Can't we be friends?"

Brenda jumped up from the bench and came close to her. "I'm not jealous and I don't want to be your friend," she yelled, stomping her foot.

Annalisa wanted to move away, but didn't want Brenda to think she was scared. She stood her ground, although her heart beat so hard she could hardly breathe. "You haven't said a kind word to me since you moved here in seventh grade. Why?"

Brenda glared at her for a moment, then blurted out, "I'm glad your parents died!" It was like a knife that hit the target, and Annalisa gasped and pressed her hands over her heart.

Just then Todd walked up and stood next to Annalisa. "Brenda, what a cruel thing to say! It's no wonder you have no friends." Brenda seemed startled, then stomped away.

Annalisa sighed.

"Never mind, Todd, she always treats me that way," Annalisa said quietly, wiping her eyes. "Let's just walk on and forget her comments. I'm hoping that if I don't react in anger, she'll change her ways. I wish I knew how to help her be happier."

"Why do you want to help someone who's unkind to you?" Todd asked.

They walked towards the school as Annalisa considered how to answer. "I want to follow the ways of Jesus. He said to love even those who are not kind to you. For me, that means to be kind to Brenda, even though she isn't kind to me."

"I know Jesus said that, but it's so hard," said Todd.

"Yes, that's for sure. But God will give grace and strength, so I can be kind even if she isn't. As Grandma used to say, "You win more friends with honey than with vinegar."

"You're right." Todd smiled approvingly at Annalisa. With that said, they arrived at school and parted to go to their classes.

Annalisa had talked to each teacher the previous Monday to collect the assignments given during her second week of absence. She had plunged into the work during her study halls, noon hour, and evenings. Now that it was Friday, she was halfway through the makeup work. At the end of the day she placed the English, Social Studies, and science text books in her backpack and began to walk home. At the sidewalk in front of the school house she heard Todd and Travis call to her. She stopped and turned around, waiting.

"May we walk with you" asked Travis.

"Certainly," said Annalisa. "Don't you have football practice on Fridays?"

"No, because there's a game tonight. Will you come to it?"

"I don't know. I'm pretty tired and still have makeup work to do."

"We understand. You need to get plenty of rest, with all you're dealing with," said Travis.

"Thanks for understanding. I'll try to come to the next home game."

"Great," both of the young men answered at once. "That's next Friday, and then the following Friday is homecoming," Todd added.

She smiled weakly. "Already?"

"Annalisa, we're glad you consented to be a friend with us," Travis said. He relieved her of her book bag and slung it over his right shoulder. Now he looked like a balanced pack horse, with his own bag on his left shoulder. "Maybe we can help you handle Brenda. Todd told me about your difficulty with her this morning," said Travis.

"Yes, she can be difficult, but she has never physically harmed me, only her comments do. I've heard that people who act like that are maybe afraid, or hurting deep down inside. It could be that moving here in seventh grade was hard for her. Maybe she had to leave friends behind and could not make any new friends here."

"Maybe she is scared of something, or had a really bad experience before coming here," said Todd. "There could be many reasons for acting as she does."

"I suppose it's easiest to ignore her, but that won't solve her problem," said Travis.

"I know," said Annalisa. "I think we need to be kind to her and include her in something. I think that deep down inside of her there is a nice, sweet girl trying to get out. I'd like to help her. Will you pray with me about it?"

"If enough people treat her with kindness, maybe she'll change," said Todd. "I'll pray for her and for you, Annalisa."

"So will I," said Travis. "What can we include her in?"

"How about the youth group at church? You two guys could talk to some of the guys and ask them to pray, too.

Suggest to them: "Say 'hello' if you pass her in the hall. If she drops her books, help her pick them up, hold a door open for her." I'll tell you what she says after I talk to her and invite her to youth group. But meanwhile, let's all be kind to her."

By this time, they had arrived at Annalisa's home and Travis put her book bag on the porch. She waved good bye to Todd and Travis. "Thanks for walking with me. See you later."

Aunt Catherine was not at home, so Annalisa sat down at her desk and started to work on her assignments. First she read the pages assigned for Social Studies, and answered the questions on the work sheet. She worked on the map of Egypt for Geography class, filling in the land forms, rivers, lakes, and agriculture areas. She colored the Nile River and the Red Sea blue.

Annalisa was just finishing this assignment when she heard a door open and close downstairs. Soon Aunt Catherine looked around her bedroom door. "Hi, Annalisa, how was school today?"

"School went well, but I did have another confrontation with Brenda before school." She told her aunt about the incident and about Todd appearing at just the right moment.

"What do you think is her problem?" asked Aunt Catherine.

"I don't know. She moved here in seventh grade and has been mean to me ever since. I don't know much about her family or where she moved from."

"From what you said about the incident today, it sounds like the girl is jealous," said Aunt Catherine, sitting down on the bed.

"Right. That's what I think, too. She thinks I'm favored by the teachers over other students."

"Teachers do appreciate students like you who take learning seriously and work hard on their assignments."

"Sometimes she says I cheat on tests and on my homework."

"Do you?"

"Aunt Catherine, of course I don't cheat! I earn every grade I receive." Annalisa's eyes began to sting and she asked, "You do believe me don't you?"

"Of course I believe you; I just wanted to hear you say it. So since you know you don't cheat, don't let it bother you that she says you do." Placing her arms around her niece, Catherine hugged her. "Honey, other people can be cruel, especially when they are jealous or their home life is not so good. Maybe her parents require too much of her or ridicule her because of something in her body or her complexion, or her interests."

"She's a bit overweight, but not much. She has blotches of acne on her face. Her clothing is out of style, and she doesn't seem to care about school or learning," Annalisa said.

"Poor girl. Maybe she's depressed."

"I'd like to help her, but she said she doesn't want my friendship. Todd overheard Brenda say she was glad my parents died." Annalisa felt a pang in her heart as she remembered, and tears trickled down her cheeks.

"What did Todd say when he heard that?" Catherine asked, offering her a tissue.

"He told her off. He said that was a cruel thing to say and no wonder she doesn't have friends. After school Todd and Travis walked me home and both said I should just treat her with kindness and respect and also pray for her."

Catherine gently lifted Annalisa's chin with her finger. "You are a lovely girl and I'm so proud of you. I hope you'll continue to be kind, respectful, and patient with Brenda. It may take a while but, when she learns you sincerely care for her and want to help her, she will change."

"I'll try; she may be a hard one to win over. Oh, one more thing---this really puzzled me. She said I was dressed 'fit to kill,' then asked, 'Whose dreams are you going to kill today?' What could she mean by that?"

"Why, I don't know. Has she had some dreams killed by someone?"

"She came to Gardenia a little more than three years ago, in seventh grade, and has seemed to hate me ever since. I can't think of anything I've done to deserve that."

Aunt Catherine shook her head, puzzled. "Let's pray for her daily, asking God for help. He always answers prayers of humble people. Live your life above reproach. Treat Brenda the way Jesus treated those with whom He came into contact. Remember his prayer on the cross?"

"Father, forgive them for they know not what they are doing?"

Catherine nodded. "Try to act the same way." Then Catherine stood up. "Now you may continue your homework while I fix supper. We can talk more while we eat."

Brenda Seeks Help

Brenda did not feel a bit proud of herself. She kept seeing the look on Annalisa's face as she clutched her heart as if a knife had lodged there. She felt almost like a murderer. *How could I have said such cruel things?*

As soon as she reached the school, she went to Mrs. Hoffman's office. "I'm sorry," the secretary said, "Mrs. Hoffman called in sick again this morning."

Brenda slumped against the counter.

The secretary added, in a hopeful tone of voice, "She did say she's better and hoped to be here on Monday. Shall I write you down for an appointment?"

"Yes," Brenda said. "I think she's expecting me to eat lunch with her on Monday and talk then. Please tell her I'm planning on it."

Brenda's head ached. Would this day never end? How could she wait until Monday? Todd's words kept going through her mind: *"Brenda, what a cruel thing to say! It's no wonder you have no friends."*

*I don't deserve friends. I don't even deserve to live. I don't know what's the sense of living anyway.*These thoughts kept going through her mind until the long day finally ended. After walking home to an empty house, she searched the medicine cabinet for something to take to kill herself with, but all she could find was one sleeping pill and a couple aspirin. *Oh well. Maybe I can at least get rid of my headache.* She took both the sleeping pill and aspirin, ate a sandwich and went to sleep. Later, she vaguely felt her mother trying to wake her, saying it was time to practice, but she ignored her and her mother gave up. After a good long night's sleep, her headache was gone and she felt better. Her mother had left a note saying, "I have to work today so I need you to do the housework. Don't neglect your practicing."

Yes, Mother. You could have at least signed it, "Love, Mom" couldn't you? But no, that would be too out of character, wouldn't it?

Yet, Brenda was relieved her mother wasn't home. At least that way they would not have arguments. While she ate breakfast, she read a homework assignment. Then she hurried to do some cleaning, at least the most essential, then threw a load of clothes into the washing machine. She did another homework assignment, and practiced an hour. She knew her mother would insist on her practicing more after she got home, so Brenda decided the homework was the biggest priority now.

"Yea, I'm almost done with Monday's assignments." she punched the air, just as she heard her mother drive into the driveway. She hurried to the piano and started to play just as her mother walked in the door.

"Boy, what a day! I'm so tired," her mother said, as she took off her coat. She sat down in the recliner to listen, and promptly fell asleep.

An hour later, after Brenda had quit practicing, her mother was still asleep. *Maybe I haven't been as grateful as I should be for her hard work in supporting us.* She found a box of macaroni and cheese and had it ready to eat by the time her mother woke up. By bedtime she had a new thought, *I guess we can get along better if I try to be more considerate.*

The next day it was more difficult to get along since her mother was home all day. But Brenda kept thinking about the words of Annalisa and Todd: *"Brenda, why are you so sarcastic? Are you sarcastic to everyone?"* and *"Brenda, what a cruel thing to say! It's no wonder you have no friends."* She didn't want to be like that anymore, so she tried hard not to react to her mother's complaining and demands as she went through the motions of the day's activities.

Monday morning, Mrs. Hoffman met Brenda in the hall before first class. "I'm so sorry I couldn't be here Thursday and Friday to talk with you, Brenda," she said, in a warm voice.

Brenda felt a stirring of hope. It felt so good to have someone smile at her. "Will it be all right to eat lunch with you today?" she asked.

"Absolutely. I'm planning on it." With a smile, she waved and walked away.

"See you then," Brenda said, and went into the classroom. She felt her face heat up when she saw Annalisa sitting at her desk. She felt like the whole class was hearing her cruel words.

At noon, Brenda set her lunch on the school counselor's desk. "Mrs. Hoffman," she said, looking and sounding defeated, "I don't do life too well and I need help."

"Brenda, that is exactly the place to start getting help—admitting you need it. I am proud of you, because it is not easy to admit that."

Brenda breathed a long sigh of relief. It felt like she'd knocked on a door, afraid she wouldn't be admitted, then the one who opened the door welcomed her with open arms.

Mrs. Hoffman took a few bites of her microwave dinner. "Tell me what's been going on with you since we talked last Monday? Have you still been feeling all stirred up inside?"

Brenda ignored the tears now running down her cheeks. "Yes. It's been a rough week. As you know, I'd been sick so I had two weeks of homework to catch up on. But my mother insisted I get back to the schedule of practicing piano four hours a day. By the time I did that, I was so tired I couldn't stay awake to do homework. I not only couldn't do the makeup work, but couldn't even do the daily work. I even flunked a spelling quiz."

"Are you still far behind?"

"I got a lot done this weekend. At least I have the current assignments done, but still not the makeup work."

"I will talk to your teachers and ask them to give you a little more time. And I'll request you take the spelling quiz over. In fact, if you don't mind, I would like to call your mother in to talk with the principal and myself about her excessive expectations about your piano practice. Is that agreeable with you?"

Brenda thought about that. Would her mother be more angry toward her afterward? But then, did it matter if she was? It was nearly unbearable this way. Besides, she felt she could trust Mrs. Hoffman to do what was best. Finally she nodded to Mrs. Hoffman. "Yes, go ahead." Mrs. Hoffman wrote herself a note.

Brenda cleared her throat. She wiped her eyes, but it did no good. "I've done something terrible," she blurted out.

Surprised, Mrs. Hoffman looked up. "What is it?"

"I told Annalisa I was glad her parents died. Brenda was crying full force now.

"Can you tell me what led up to this?"

"After I had such trouble with the schoolwork, and seeing how easy it was for her to catch up, I felt so jealous and angry. Then I had a nightmare. I'd had this nightmare before, but this time Annalisa was in it. There was chaos and confusion, yelling and doors slamming. I was dressed up to go somewhere with my dad, but I couldn't find him. Then Annalisa found the map of how to find him, but she wouldn't give it to me. By Friday morning, I felt like Annalisa was my enemy. I was sitting on a bench resting when Annalisa came around that hedge just before the school. She was dressed so cute, and I was jealous all over again. First I called her a "spiffy princess," meaning it almost as a compliment, but then I said her name in a nasty way and asked "Is this how you 'dress to kill?' Whose dreams are you going to kill today? Or are you just dressed nice so you'll dazzle the teachers into giving you 'A's?"

Mrs. Hoffman sat back in her chair. "How did she react?"

"She asked if I'm sarcastic to everyone and why and that she's sorry I'm jealous. Then, she really surprised me by suggesting we be friends. I couldn't believe it."

The counselor looked at her notes from the previous talk. "Didn't you tell me last week that you'd like to be friends with her?"

"Yes, but that morning I was in such a bad mood, I hated the idea of it. Then she had to bring up seventh grade---"

"What happened in seventh grade?"

"The summer before, my mother and I moved here and I started school here. When she mentioned seventh grade, I thought of what happened, and what she did, and I just got so angry that before I knew it, I'd blurted out 'I'm glad your parents died.' Annalisa looked shocked and pressed her hands over her heart as if a knife had gone into it. Just then Todd walked up and said to me, 'Brenda, what a cruel thing to say! It's no wonder you have no friends.' I feel really bad about saying it now."

Mrs. Hoffman sent a note to Brenda's next class asking that she be excused, and they talked for another hour. Brenda poured out her heart about events and feelings from before seventh grade and on to the present and the counselor gave her encouragement. When Brenda left the counselor's office, she felt more hopeful than she could remember ever feeling. She also felt lighter and cleaner.

18

Going Through The Motions

The next few days after the confrontation went by quite uneventfully for Annalisa. She noticed that the excruciating pain of grief seemed to be dulling a little, but she felt like she was just going through the motions of living, rather than really living, as she did homework, attended church, school, grief support group, and youth group.

The only time Annalisa felt totally interested in anything was when she prayed for Brenda. *"Father, Brenda seems so miserable. Show me how to help her."* She asked the other girls in Youth Group to pray for her, also.

She still talked frequently to Mary Lou, her best friend, on the phone or by email or text, but she sensed Mary Lou didn't have the same depth of concern for Brenda. Neither did Mary Lou seem to understand Annalisa's concern for Brenda or the depth of Annalisa's grief.

For some reason, Lord, I sense Brenda could understand my grief if we could get close and talk about it. I wonder what she has experienced that was so hard? Please, Lord, will you show me how to reach her and help her?

After praying, Annalisa felt the 'peace that passes all understanding' again. She also felt a particular closeness to her parents, because she got the feeling this is how they felt about the people in Ecuador, wanting to help them know Jesus in order to be happier.

The Leak

"Annalisa, do you mind if I sort through and rearrange the spare room?" Catherine asked after school one day. "I need more space to put my things from my apartment."

"No, I don't mind. We hardly ever used that room. It's just an extra bedroom and storage area." She finished her snack and worked on her homework. Catherine had picked her up from school because it was raining.

Soon, Annalisa heard Catherine exclaim, "Oh no! This is not good. We need to repair this as soon as possible."

"What needs to be repaired?"

"There must be a hole in the roof because water is dripping into this room and has ruined the spread on the bed. I'm sure the mattress is water-soaked and maybe ruined, also,---maybe even the carpet."

"I'll get some buckets." Annalisa quickly found some. "Let's move the bed and we'll set buckets to catch the water." When that was done, Annalisa said, "Aunt Catherine, let's call Zeke Vander Broek and ask him to come and see what needs to be done. I know he said on a sympathy card to call him if we needed any handyman jobs done."

"What kind of work does he do?"

"He's a building contractor."

Soon after the phone call, Zeke appeared and examined the ceiling. "Hmm." As he lifted the mattress, they saw water stains on the box spring and underneath. "Hmm," Zeke said, again.

Taking out his pocket knife, he cut a slit in the carpet. Again he uttered a soft "Hmm," then asked, "Where's the attic?" They showed him where to get into the attic. He went up there and did some pounding. When he came down, he turned to Catherine and said, "When the rain stops, I'll come back." He stopped; a shade of red began to creep up his neck. "Th-then I can fix the hole." He turned quickly and raced out the door.

"Hmm. He's a man of few words, isn't he?" Annalisa remarked with a little smile.

"Yes, poor man. I suppose he's so distraught over the death of his wife…"

"What?" Annalisa stared at her in surprise.

"Yes, Phyliss…Phyliss Vander Broek." She picked up a bulletin and pointed out the name to Annalisa. "Remember, we saw him at the 'families of the deceased' prayer meeting?"

"But Aunt Catherine, that's his sister. See?" She pointed to the obituary. "He's never been married. Oh look," she pointed to the bucket. "The dripping stopped, though it's still raining."

The next morning, the sun shone in all its glory. Zeke appeared early with a ladder, bucket of roofing tar, a few shingles, nails and hammer. They watched him start the job.

As he started up the ladder, Aunt Catherine pleaded, "Zeke, be careful on the roof."

He paused in his climbing, his eyes met hers, and he blushed. "Hmm," he said with a smile and a nod, and continued up the ladder. Soon a single shingle fell from the roof. Annalisa could smell the tar and hear pounding. Then he went inside and carried out the damaged mattress and box spring and set it by the curb, as Catherine had requested. He cut open the carpet and showed her how badly that was damaged. He stood up and asked, "New carpet?"

"Annalisa, what do you think?" Catherine asked, as they looked at the damaged carpet. "Should we patch it, or tear it all out and purchase new carpet?"

"Or if there is a nice hardwood floor, we could varnish it and buy a big area rug."

"That's a good idea, Annalisa." Catherine sounded pleased.

"Be back after lunch," Zeke said, and left.

"I'm going to school now, Aunt Catherine. It's a beautiful day to walk." Annalisa enjoyed her walk in the sunshine. *That Zeke seems like a sweet fellow. I wonder if he has a romantic interest in Aunt Catherine. It sure would be nice to have a man around the house.* She felt a pain in her chest again, as she thought, *I sure miss Dad.*

After school, Catherine told Annalisa about the afternoon. "When Zeke returned, he repaired the ceiling and tore out the carpet, placing it, the discarded ceiling tiles, and the old shingles in a large dumpster he'd brought along. He stuffed the damaged mattress and box spring in it, also. When he returned to the house to pick up his tools, I offered him freshly baked cookies and coffee. When he took the first bite, his face lighted up with a smile and he looked at me and said, "Hmmm."

She blushed. Annalisa snickered.

"After three more cookies and two cups of coffee, he left, waving goodbye. I called to him saying, "Wait, Zeke. How much do we owe you?" He only shook his head and waved again."

She sat with her chin in her hands, gazing into space. Presently, she looked at Annalisa. "Shall we go downtown now and price carpet and area rugs?"

"I have youth group tonight and homework. Could we do it tomorrow after school?"

"Yes, that would be fine. That will give me time to clean up the room first."

At supper, Catherine said, "It bothers me that Zeke didn't leave us a bill yet. I wonder how much he will charge. Do you know him well, Annalisa?"

"He goes to our church. He always sits near the front on the left hand side. I know he does a lot of handyman jobs for people. I also noticed that, at the potluck at church that first Sunday you were here, he watched what you put on the table and then took seconds only from what you brought." She grinned at her blushing aunt.

"Well, I never…. Now you stop your giggling, Annalisa."

Annalisa left for youth group with Todd and Travis. They had picked up her friend, Mary Lou already. Annalisa told her about Catherine and Zeke, and they snickered together in the back seat. At the meeting, Annalisa still felt a little like she stood out like a sore thumb because everyone was so sorry for her in the loss of her parents. It was not as bad as the first time back on the 13th. That time she appreciated their concern, but felt uncomfortable and it almost made her wish she hadn't come.

The next afternoon, after shopping for half an hour, Catherine and Annalisa bought some floor varnish and a beautiful large area rug in shades of brown and blue. As they were leaving the store, they met Zeke coming in. He tipped his hat with a slight smile.

Catherine smiled back. "We bought varnish and an area rug for that room," she told him.

"I'll help tomorrow," he said, then quickly turned on his heel and left. Catherine stood there with her mouth open, then said to Annalisa, "I didn't ask him to help. I was going to do it myself."

Annalisa just smiled, and said "Hmm."

Halfway home, Aunt Catherine asked her, "Would you stop giggling, please?"

Friday morning, Zeke arrived just as Annalisa was leaving for school. Annalisa said to Catherine, "Have fun at your varnishing party, Hmm?"

Her aunt snapped her with the dish towel. "Hmm yourself. Get off to school with you now."

Annalisa walked down the front walk, then waved as she turned toward school. Catherine waved back.

She soon met up with Todd and Travis after walking a block and then walked with them. "I can't believe the weather has still been so pleasant," said Travis. "It won't be long now before the snow flies."

That evening, Annalisa asked her aunt, "How did the varnishing party go this morning?

"Oh yes; come ---let me show you." She led her to the spare room and opened the door.

"Wow!" said Annalisa. "Did you already finish the whole room? It looks beautiful!"

"Yes, it just needs to dry now, and then we'll put down our new area rug. Zeke brought an electric sander and as soon as he had sanded one section, I varnished it. I was surprised how fast it went. Now let's eat before supper gets cold."

After they'd prayed and begun eating, Annalisa asked, "So was the sander the only sound at this party? Hmm?"

"Of course he had to give me directions, but he didn't say much while we worked. We were finished by noon, so I gave him some soup for lunch."

Annalisa's eyes grew wide. "You did? Did he say anything during lunch?"

"Oh yes. We had a good conversation." Aunt Catherine quickly got up to go to the cupboard. She stood there a minute, as if forgetting what she was after, then came back with the salt. She looked like she might have been out in the sun for awhile.

Resuming her meal, Annalisa asked, "What did you talk about?"

"Oh, he told me about his childhood, and his job, and so forth."

"He did? How long did he stay? After you were done with the work, I mean?"

Aunt Catherine cleared her throat, smiled a little, then said, "A couple hours."

Annalisa stared with her mouth open for many seconds, watching her aunt's face turn pink. "Well, Aunt Catherine, I'm glad you had a good time." She smiled and gave her a hug. "I better go work on homework some more before I go to the game. Thank you for supper."

"You're welcome, Dear."

Annalisa paused on her way upstairs. "Aunt Catherine, would you like to go to the game with me?"

"Why thank you, Dear. I might. I'll think about it."

Later, as Annalisa worked on her English assignment, she could hear her aunt singing as she did the dishes. She took time out from her reading to comment to herself, *That sounds good. I'm glad Aunt Catherine is happy. These last few weeks have been hard on her, as well as me.* She chewed on her pencil absentmindedly. *I used to sing a lot around the house. But now I only sing in church, it seems.* Then she had a new idea. *Maybe I would feel better if I make myself sing, rather than waiting until I feel like it. Many songs do feel like a balm to my soul.*

Later, Catherine peeked in at her again. "Are you watching the clock? Isn't it almost time to go to the game?"

Annalisa looked up at the clock. "Oh! It is! That time has flown by." Are you coming with me, Auntie?"

"Yes, I would enjoy that. I'll go get my coat on."

Annalisa felt grateful her aunt came along. Otherwise, it would have been too easy to feel sad that her parents couldn't come with her to games like before. The crowd became quite excited as the home team pulled ahead in the second half. The score kept getting tied---then Todd made a touchdown, after running 80 yards, and won the game. She sent him a text after the team went to the locker room: "U wer grt! Congrats on TD. Ant n I r going home now."

The next week, Mr. Pendleton, the band director, sent for Annalisa to see him.

"The school's choir director has mentioned to me about your musical abilities and talent. I would like you to consider joining the school band."

"Thank you, Mr. Pendleton, but my schedule is full this fall, and I've never taken an instrument or lessons other than piano."

"I would give you lessons at no cost after school once a week. If you come tonight, we'll try various instruments and see which interest you and which you feel comfortable with. Then you can be ready to start band next semester."

Annalisa struggled a little with her decision. It would probably be fun to be in band. But she replied, "Thank you again, but as I said, my schedule is full this year. I don't believe I should take on any more right now. Maybe next summer I'll consider it for next year."

"I understand. We can talk again before summer and decide whether you want summer lessons or not and if so, choose an instrument then."

"Thank you, Mr. Pendleton."

"You're welcome, Annalisa. I'll be glad to have you in band next year if you decide so."

At lunch that Wednesday, Annalisa sat across from Todd and Travis. Between bites, she told them about the conversation with the school band director. "But I just don't think I should take on anything more right now. My class schedule is full with lots of homework; I still have makeup work to do; I'm going to Grief Support Group on Tuesdays; Wednesday night is youth group. Some days I need to go to the library to do homework after school."

Travis nodded. "That sounds like a wise, mature decision. I'm sure Mr. Pendleton was thinking of the joy of being in band and that it would help you with your grief, which is true. However, grief work takes up a lot of emotional energy and you need time to think and process things. So it is not a good idea to overload yourself. Some people try to get so busy they don't have time to think or be lonesome, but that only prolongs the grief."

"You sound like a wise man, Travis Klein. How did you learn so much before even graduating from high school?"

Travis laughed gently. Then he got serious again. He and Todd exchanged meaningful looks. "I told you my grief event happened eight years ago," Travis said. "I was only ten that fall and so devastated I didn't want to think. My Dad had gotten me into some healthy things like Little League and basketball and track and softball, but when Mom died, he and I both closed ourselves off from people. When I was home, I filled my thoughts with video games or TV or anything to keep from thinking. When my Dad got home from work, he was so exhausted and depressed, he didn't talk to me much. Since I thought all my teammates still had both their parents, I was so jealous of them I couldn't relate to them. I felt all alone."

"That winter I fell apart and tried to commit suicide. It was unsuccessful, but then people realized I needed help. I was out of school the rest of that year because of it, so I had to repeat fourth grade."

Todd interjected, "That's why he's older than most of the seniors."

Travis nodded then continued, "The school counselor came to visit me in the hospital, while I was recovering, and she arranged for professional counseling. I talked with this Dr. Turnagin many times when we still lived in southern Iowa. After we moved here to Gardenia, in northwestern Iowa, I talked with Mrs. Hoffman and Pastor Brady, too. Meanwhile, the extensive counseling I had received from Dr. T. helped so much that I began thinking I wanted to become a psychiatrist. When I had a chance, the summer I was sixteen, to take the extensive training to help others, I jumped at the chance."

Annalisa listened intently. She appreciated that Travis would share this with her. When they finished lunch, they took their trays to the conveyor belt.

"We'll walk home with you, after football practice is over, if you wish. We understand you are planning to go to the library to study." said Todd.

"Yes," said Annalisa. "I'll meet you by the front door at 4:30."

"Speaking of football," Travis said, "Can you come to the game this Friday night? It will be Homecoming." They all walked to class as they talked.

"Yes, I will. Catherine and I enjoyed the one last week. Maybe she would like to ask Zeke to come this time."

"Good."

20

The Rest of the Todd &Travis Story

On the way home after football practice, Annalisa took the initiative to continue their conversation. "Both of you are so kind to me. Why?"

"As we told you," Todd said, "each of us has lost a parent. We know how hard it is emotionally for a long time. After losing your parents, we think you need a couple of good friends."

"You're right," said Annalisa. Her eyes shone with sudden tears. "I miss them so much." The tears flowed down her cheeks, and Todd gave her a clean tissue. "Do you think I will ever be able to think about them without crying like a baby?"

"Sure you will; it will take a while, but there will come a time when you can think about them without crying," said Travis.

"Meanwhile," Todd added, "There's nothing wrong with crying. I've heard it actually helps---that crying has a healing effect."

"You'll always miss them," Travis said, "but sometime in the future you'll become used to the fact that they are gone and you'll adjust to that and go on with your life."

"Remember," said Todd, "we are your friends and we care about you. We'll listen whenever you need someone to talk to."

Annalisa felt grateful for these friends. "What grade were each of you in when you lost your parent and how did it happen?" Annalisa asked.

"I was in fifth grade when my mother died of cancer," said Travis. "She'd been sick for eight months, gradually getting worse and worse. My Dad became depressed during her illness. Although he took good care of her until she died, he didn't seem to have any energy left to help me deal with it."

"And a year later," said Todd, "when I was in fourth grade, my dad got killed in a hunting accident. Our remaining parents are brother and sister. By this time, Travis had had the suicide episode. Our parents decided to move here to Gardenia and buy the duplex together so we could live next door to each other. That way my mom could look out for him while his dad worked. It was a rough time for all of us and we cried a lot, too. But I think it brought us closer together."

"A couple of years later," added Travis, "our surviving parents each found a friend. They fell in love and married, but we kept on living in the duplex."

"Meanwhile, some kids said cruel things to us and we both punched a few kids out. I would not recommend doing that. We learned to consider the source of a cruel comment and turn around and ignore the cruel person. When we did that, they soon stopped."

Todd touched Annalisa's arm and said in a hushed tone, "Speaking of which, here comes Brenda. Be careful how you respond to her."

"Well," said Brenda, hands on hips, "here's the orphan. Haven't they sent you to an orphanage yet?"

Annalisa met her gaze, trying to understand her thoughts. "No, I have my Aunt living with me and do not need to go to an orphanage."

Brenda just stood there, and Annalisa couldn't think of anything else to say.

Finally Todd spoke up. "Bye, Brenda. We are on our way,"

"I'll pray for you, Brenda," said Annalisa.

"What good will that do? If God is so good, why did your parents die?" sneered Brenda.

Annalisa felt like a club had hit her in the chest. She didn't answer.

Travis said, "What has turned you against God, Brenda? He loves you and can help you."

"Ha, God doesn't exist and I've gotten along without Him for sixteen years. I don't need Him even if He does exist." Brenda scowled. It seemed like a dark cloud hovered over her.

With that, Todd, Travis, and Annalisa turned and walked away. After a few silent minutes, Annalisa said, "I feel sad for Brenda. She has no friends because she is so cruel and negative to everyone. Do you suppose she doesn't know how to make and keep friends?"

"We don't know her circumstances. I wonder--- does she even want help?" asked Travis.

"I think she wants friends, but doesn't know how to make them. I believe she can be a good person, but has been so rude to people for so long that no one wants to associate with her. Let's pray for her and maybe we can help her."

"Good idea, Annalisa," said Todd. "God still works miracles. You may be the one He uses to reach Brenda and to help her realize she needs a Savior." They prayed aloud together.

Soon Annalisa saw her two-story ranch-style home on Delft Wege (Wege means 'Way' in Dutch, Annalisa remembered her dad saying). From a block away, the sight of the front of the house made her feel happy and grateful to live there. Three gables peered at her above a porch roof which extended the length of the sunshine yellow house trimmed in white. It had a three stall garage, and a red brick sidewalk leading to the street. Her dad had done beautiful landscaping with different kinds of shrubs, colorful flowers, and trees on the corner lot.

"Here we are at my house. I'd invite you in for some milk and cookies, but my Aunt is out applying for a job and, since I do not see her car in the driveway, I assume she is still out. Thanks for walking me home, Todd and Travis."

"We will see you tonight." said Travis. Todd smiled and waved.

Todd and Travis walked down the block toward their home and Annalisa let herself into her house, and placed her books on her desk in her room. *Aunt Catherine has been so good to me, and I love her so much. I think I'll start our dinner for tonight.* She changed into some comfortable sweats and washed her hands. She peeled and cut up potatoes and put them on the burner on low, then washed a head of broccoli before starting her homework at the table.

Soon she heard her Aunt Catherine enter the house. Annalisa anticipated her surprise. "What a sweetheart! You've started supper," she exclaimed. She hugged Annalisa.

"You are so good to me. I wanted to find some small way to thank you."

"Thank you," Catherine said. "I would have left a note, but I thought I'd be home before you. I found a job and they said I could start immediately. I already worked half a day."

"You did?" Annalisa thought her aunt looked especially happy.

"Yes, I'm working for a publishing house here in town. Write By Inspiration." Catherine grinned. "They'll give me special training, and I can do some work at home whenever I want to."

"Oh, Aunt Catherine, how nice. What will you be doing?"

"I'll be reading manuscripts, doing an initial screening on submissions. Also, on accepted manuscripts, I'll be looking for grammatical errors, spelling errors, mistakes in punctuation, and other errors. I'll be called a copy editor."

"How do you know about publishing, Aunt Catherine?"

"I don't know much, but I did major in English Literature in college. Before you were born, I once wrote a book, a love story, and it was published. Then I had to get a "real job" and didn't have time for writing any more."

"Do you have a copy of the book?"

"Not here with me, but I'll look through your parents' library. They may still have the copy I gave to them."

"Oh, good. I enjoy reading love stories," said Annalisa.

As they talked, Catherine checked the potatoes, and looked in the freezer. "How about frozen fish to add to this. Does that sound good?"

"Yes, that's fine. I have homework to read for American History and a few English sentences to do. The band director invited me to join the band, but I told him I'm too busy now."

"That's a wise decision. Thanks for peeling the potatoes. I'll call when dinner's ready."

Annalisa said, "You're welcome," and went up the stairs to her room. The English assignment was easy. Just twenty sentences in which she needed to place the proper punctuation in each sentence. The American History assignment was to read a chapter in the text book about Paul Revere's ride. She'd just finished the chapter when her Aunt Catherine called, "Annalisa, come downstairs, dinner is ready to be served."

"This smells delicious," she said as she looked at the attractive table with its steamed broccoli, fish, mashed potatoes, rolls, and water."

"You can thank me by helping with the dishes," said Aunt Catherine with a smile.

"Aw, you just ruined my day," laughed Annalisa. "No, just kidding. I'm glad to help."

"You just made my day, young lady."

While they did dishes, they discussed the events of the day.

"Classes were good, and I've already completed my homework for tomorrow. Did you read any interesting manuscripts today?"

"Yes, I read one about a boy in third grade who says he does not like school because some classmates are picking on him and badgering him. The proposal is for a picture book. Anyway, the boy's Mother and Father help him learn how to deal with his classmates. The end of the story tells how the boy begins to get along better in school and make friends."

"That sounds like a good book for grade school students. Maybe we need one for high schoolers, also," Annalisa said, thinking of Brenda.

Catherine said, "I was going to read a book tonight, but I'm tired of reading."

"I wonder why," said Annalisa with a smile.

"I think I'll watch TV while you are at youth group," said Aunt Catherine.

Annalisa turned to go to her room, then looked back at her aunt. "Would you like to go to the Homecoming game with me this Friday?"

"Why yes, that would be fun. We had a good time last week."

"Could you invite Zeke along?"

Catherine blushed. "Maybe, if he calls."

An hour later, Annalisa put on her coat just as they heard Travis and Todd drive up.

"I'll see you around nine. Bye."

When she returned, Annalisa felt exhausted. She climbed the stairs to her room, changed into her night clothing and softly padded down the stairs to say good night to her Aunt. "I'm going to bed Aunt Catherine. It's been a long day."

"Okay Dear. Bye the way, Zeke did call and would be glad to go with us Friday."

Annalisa smiled, kissed her aunt and said goodnight. She went upstairs, brushed her teeth and her hair and, after reading a Psalm in her Bible, prayed for her aunt, her friends, and Brenda. "Help her learn how to make friends and treat others with kindness. Help me to treat Brenda with kindness and respect. Help her to see you living in me." After turning off her bedside light, Annalisa was soon asleep.

21

A Breakthrough

*O*h no, thought Annalisa. *I don't feel up to this right now. Help me, Lord.* She had just come from a session with Margery and she had gotten quite emotional as they talked. Annalisa felt drained, and knew her eyes were red from crying. As she stood at the corner, waiting for the traffic light to change, she watched Brenda walking toward her.

"Hello, Orphan," said Brenda in a snotty voice. "Have you been crying on someone's shoulder again? When are you going to get over your parents' dying?"

"Hello, Brenda," said Annalisa, trying to speak in a kind voice. "Yes, I have been crying. It's part of the grief process, according to the counselor I just saw. She also said I'll never quit missing my parents, but in time it won't hurt so much. I'll adjust to them being gone and go on with my life. In the meantime, I have friends."

Annalisa prayed for courage, swallowed, and took the plunge. "Brenda, I'd like you to be my friend, also."

"Huh?" Brenda stared at her with her mouth open.

"Yes, Brenda. I'm sure you want friends, too, but probably have trouble making and keeping friends." The signal light changed to 'go' so Annalisa said "Let's go" and started across.

Brenda ran to catch up and walk beside Annalisa. "I think you've been seeing too many counselors, and now you think you're one, too," said Brenda.

"No, Brenda. I just know everyone needs friends so they're not so lonely, and I haven't seen you with other people. You're always alone. I haven't seen you smile or laugh. Besides, God said to do unto others as you would want them to do unto you. If we could become friends we could benefit each other. You know--- I help you and you help me."

"There you go with that God thing again. I've told you I don't believe in God. He hasn't done anything for me." They both were silent until they stepped up on the curb on the other side.

Annalisa stopped and looked at her, and silently prayed about what to say. "What did you want him to do for you, Brenda?" Annalisa asked, quietly.

"What?" Brenda looked startled.

She searched Brenda's eyes. "What did you ask God for that he didn't give you?"

Brenda looked down at her feet. She didn't say anything for several moments. Meanwhile they began walking again. After half a block, she glanced at Annalisa. "You know I moved here just before seventh grade, right?"

"Yes, I remember that."

"My mother and I came alone. Daddy had given up on the marriage. She was always nagging at him to do this or that. They got a divorce shortly after."

Annalisa stopped and looked at her. "Oh Brenda, I'm so sorry! I suspected something had happened to make you so unhappy."

"I had a couple friends there" she continued, "but since we had to move, I lost contact with them. I was too unhappy to write to them, or anything." She gazed off into the distance.

Annalisa sent up an arrow prayer. *Jesus, help her. Tell me what to say.* "Brenda, God loves you and wants to be your friend." She put a hand on Brenda's arm.

Brenda recoiled at the touch and pulled away. "No! He does not love me! If God loved me, he would have changed my mother's attitude and stopped the divorce! He would have kept my Daddy from committing suicide!"

Annalisa stared open-mouthed at Brenda while Brenda glared at her, then burst into tears. Annalisa stepped closer and put her arms around Brenda. "You poor dear," she murmured. "Now I understand why you are so unhappy." She held her tight while Brenda sobbed the past away.

When Brenda calmed down, Annalisa said to her, "Brenda, I really would like to be your friend. And if you come to my youth group, I'll introduce you to some other really nice teenagers. If you allow us to help you, I think we could."

"I'll think about it." Brenda looked as if she were trying to decide whether or not to jump off a high dive for the first time. "Nobody has ever said they want me as a friend.

Look at me, Annalisa. Who would ever want to be a friend to a person who is overweight, has a pizza complexion, is angry all the time, wears out of style clothing, and lives on the wrong side of the tracks?" She choked back her tears.

Annalisa spoke firmly. "Brenda, I do want to be your friend, and I think others would also if you didn't drive them away with your angry talk. Some of the girls and I, and the wife of our youth group leader, would like to help you."

"Why would you do that?"

"Because we are all Christians and, because Jesus loves us, we are able to love others. If you read the Bible you'll discover that Jesus spent most of his time with the poor people of his day, and those with problems. God loves you, Brenda, and so do I. I'll pray for you. If I give you a Bible, will you promise to read it?"

"I've never had a Bible," said Brenda.

"I would like to give one to you and help you find your way through it. Please let me do this for you. There are no strings attached, except you allow me to spend some time someday soon to guide you through some Bible verses and help you understand them. You name the day and the place, and I'll meet you there and we will talk," said Annalisa.

"Okay, a week from today, after school in the reading room at the public library uptown."

"I'll be there with your new Bible."

As they parted, Annalisa prayed, "Please, Lord, help Brenda to get to know you as you really are—a loving, merciful God who doesn't cause evil to happen. Lord, I don't understand why you allowed my parents to die, but

I do know you are good. You are holy and righteous and you know what you are doing. I trust that you know best."

She'd almost reached her house when she met Todd and Travis. "Why so pensive, m' lady?" Todd asked, with a fake English accent.

"Oh, good afternoon," she said with a smile. "I didn't see you coming."

"Is the fair maiden preoccupied?" asked Travis, also with an accent.

Annalisa smiled. "I have a request to ask of you."

"Oh, oh. The fair maiden has some sort of trickery on her mind. Be careful to what you say 'yes' dear cousin," said Travis.

"Gentlemen, and I use the term lightly," said Annalisa, "my request is that you take me to the moon in your chariot."

"We've been had. Yon fair maiden is devious," said Todd. "We're beholden to do it."

Annalisa laughed.

Bowing low, they both said, "Please forgive us for our shameless behavior. Our only excuse is the desire to hear you laugh."

"You are forgiven." Annalisa giggled. "Now, if we can be serious, my request is that you pray for me and with me for Brenda. I am going to meet with her next week at the library uptown and give her a Bible. I'll show her some verses about salvation. I've invited her to the youth group at church and I think some of us can help her if she'll allow us to. She admitted to me she has some problems she'd like to work on and wants to make a few changes in her life."

"Wow, she told you that?" Todd asked.

"Yes she did, through tear-filled eyes. I think she wants help but has no idea where to go for help. I think the girls and wives of our sponsors could help her become a new person. We need God's help and the help of some of the members of the group."

"Let's pray right now," said Todd. "Look here's a bench for us to sit upon."

Sitting between Todd and Travis, Annalisa began to pray. "Dear Father, we come to you today knowing you love Brenda as much as you love the three of us. Please help her with her problems and help her to read the Bible I'm going to give her. In Jesus name, Amen."

Travis prayed next. "Father you know all about Brenda. She's angry, has no friends, and is kind of rough and negative in her speech and attitude. Help us to help her."

Then Todd: "Father, I don't know much about Brenda, but I'm willing to help her. I think those who are angry and negative need someone to help them change their attitudes. Use me in any way you choose. Amen."

Annalisa said, "I'll continue to pray for her and will show her some verses to help her realize God loves her. I've asked God to help me know which verses to show her and how to help her. I hope others will accept her and offer their help as well."

Annalisa smiled and thanked each of the boys. "Come on gentlemen, there's a fresh batch of cookies and some milk at my house. We can sit on the back porch and chow down."

"The fair young maiden is still trying to trap us," said Travis.

"Yes," said Todd, "but what a way to go."

"You guys never quit, do you," chuckled Annalisa.

"It's so nice to hear you laugh again," said Todd and Travis in unison.

22

High School Homecoming

riday evening, Catherine, Annalisa and Zeke met Todd and Travis and their parents at a special dinner provided for the football players and their family and friends. After eating, the boys left to get suited up for the game, and the rest visited until time to go sit in the bleachers. After her initial memory tug of her parents going with her to games and other things, and the lonesome feeling that brought, Annalisa was able to enjoy the fellowship at dinner and the game. She did not feel interested in attending the Homecoming Dance, however.

School the next week started out well for Annalisa. She was able to complete all of her class assignments on time and did well on her English and History tests. From time to time she saw Brenda and was polite and kind to her in what she said and did, although Brenda was back to her old self with the bitter attitude. For example, on Monday she said:

"Hello Orphan, are you still here? I thought the state agencies would have come for you by now. Have you been flunking all your tests in your grieving?"

"Hi Brenda, I'm living with my maiden Aunt, Catherine. I have all the love and care I need and I have friends. I passed the last English and History tests with A grades."

"Yeah, I heard you cheat on tests and you are teacher's pet. They all feel sorry for you because your parents died."

"Brenda, I do not cheat on tests, I study to earn every grade I receive. I need to leave now. I'll see you at the library on Thursday where we can talk some more," said Annalisa.

"Good bye Orphan."

Walking home Annalisa began to pray silently. *"Dear Jesus, I want so much to help Brenda. I pray it is your will that I do. Please heal my pain and continue to help me be kind to her. I still think that deep down inside of her is a wonderful girl trying to rise to the surface. Help me to know her and help her change her bitter and angry attitude. I know you love Brenda as much as you do me. Help her to know it, also. In Jesus name I pray, Amen."*

Soon after Annalisa arrived home, Aunt Catherine walked in the door from the garage. "Hello, Annalisa, how was school today?" She removed her coat and hung it up in the closet.

"Hello, Aunt Catherine. School was good. On Thursday, I'm going to the public library to meet with Brenda, give her a Bible and talk with her. I'm beginning to discover why she is the way she is."

"Annalisa, are you sure you want to do that? I thought she was a bully of sorts."

"Yes, I do. I think she can become a wonderful girl. I'd like to help her dismiss that angry side of her. I'm going to invite her to go to youth group with me and meet some of the other members of the group. Maybe we can help her see her need for Jesus and become a Christian. Todd and Travis are praying for me."

"Annalisa, I am so proud of you. You could be sitting here feeling sorry for yourself, but instead you are reaching out to another girl who has a problem," said Aunt Catherine.

"You know the old adage: 'Do unto others as you would have them do unto you,'" Annalisa said, paging through a textbook. She looked up in a moment and said, "You know what? I think that this thing with Brenda is helping me understand why my parents wanted to go to the mission field."

"How's that?" asked Catherine.

"Well, it seems like God has given me this love for Brenda which I wouldn't naturally have because of the way she's acted. Because of the love He's given me, I want to help her know him. I think my parents were given that type of love by God for the people in Ecuador, because they needed it, too. I don't feel angry anymore at them for going."

Catherine nodded and smiled at Annalisa. "That's wonderful."

Annalisa shared this insight next day at the Grief Support Group meeting. They had a good discussion at this meeting, the fifth one she had attended, and she began to feel more interest in life.

That evening, Annalisa came home with the urge to cook. She laid her books on her desk in her room and went back downstairs to the kitchen. As she washed her hands, she wondered if her Aunt had made any plans for the evening meal. *I need to ask her to teach me more about cooking so I can start dinner when she works late. All I know how to do is peel potatoes.* Soon she had the potatoes ready and set them aside. Looking in the book case in the corner of the kitchen, she selected a cookbook. She paged through the book, finding many main dish recipes for beef, pork, chicken, turkey, and fish. Some recipes looked confusing: *What on earth does parboil mean? and saute, marinate, and julienne?* As she turned the pages, she found many more terms that had no meaning for her, as well. *My goodness, cooking is a complicated task. I think I'd better take a home economics class next fall. There is so much to learn and Aunt Catherine will not be with me forever. Besides, if I ever marry, I'll need to know those skills.*

When Catherine arrived home, she went to the sink for a drink of water. "What are you looking for in the cookbooks?"

"I peeled potatoes and wondered what else we could have, so I started paging through one of my Mom's cookbooks. What a confusing journey that turned out to be. I don't know what a lot of the words mean. How did you learn to cook, Aunt Catherine?"

Washing her hands, Catherine answered, "I stood next to my mother when she prepared meals and learned from her. First I just watched. As time passed and I learned more skills, she let me do some things while she did other things. I also took home economics classes in school."

"Yes, I think I will do that next year---maybe cooking in the fall and sewing in the spring," said Annalisa, putting the cookbooks away.

"Good ideas, but don't cut back on the academic classes you need for college."

"I won't. I really want to go to college."

"What would you study?" asked Aunt Catherine.

"I'm not sure. Maybe teaching, or nursing, or business so I could own a book store or a clothing shop."

"What would you teach if that were your choice?"

"I like little children; maybe kindergarten. Right now I'm just thinking of ideas. I wonder if I should take an aptitude test?"

"That would be a good idea." Catherine nodded her approval.

"What were you planning to have for dinner? Will you teach me how to fix it?"

"Why of course, ma cherie," said Aunt Catherine. She started mimicking a French chef, "M'sieur Poupon ..."

"What does that mean? He always says to use mustard?"

"At that they both laughed until tears rolled down their cheeks. Handing her Aunt a tissue, Annalisa dried her eyes on another.

"The best way I know to learn about cooking is to actually cook something," said Aunt Catherine. "You know how to start potatoes. Let them cook about fifteen minutes on medium, then test the potatoes with a fork. When the fork goes through the potatoes, you know they are done cooking because they are soft."

Annalisa nodded. "Soft potatoes are done potatoes. Got that."

"Usually, you will have already decided what kind of meat you want to eat and have it sitting out to thaw."

Catherine picked up a package of pork chops from the counter, "and you will have decided how to prepare it." She handed the package to Annalisa.

"I think I'd like baked pork chops tonight, just plain, no breading," said Annalisa, as she read the label, then opened the thawed package.

"Good choice," said Aunt Catherine, smiling. "However, I usually put the pork chops in the oven first and then start the potatoes. Since you've already started the potatoes, do you want to shut them off for awhile, or do you want to think of a quicker way to cook the pork chops?"

"I'm really hungry," said Annalisa. "Let's do them as quickly as possible."

Catherine got out a sharp knife and a cutting board. "We will cut them in strips and fry them. They would be really good with stir fry vegetables. Does that sound good to you?"

"Yes, it sure does." Annalisa took the cutting board and knife from her aunt's hands.

"Be careful. Do you know how to use that?"

"Yes, my Mom often let me help her cut vegetables."

"Well, meat is a little different to cut. It can slip easier, so go slow and hold on carefully. Cut it in strips about the size of a finger."

While she cut the meat, Catherine took bell peppers of different colors out of the freezer, and an onion out of the refrigerator drawer. "These are already cut, but I'll cut the onion. Now we put oil in the pan and let it heat to medium. When it is hot, add the meat, sprinkle it with salt and pepper and stir it around a bit. As soon as it changes color from pink to light-brown, add the peppers and onions and some Bragg's Amino Acid, put the cover on, and let it simmer on low about five minutes."

"What does simmer mean?"

"Simmer means it cooks at a very low temperature. See on the stove knob, it is this mark next to warm." She turned to look her niece in the eye. "Pork is one meat you need to be careful to cook thoroughly, since it can cause a serious illness called trichinosis. So, just before serving, cut a piece in half to see if the inside is nearly white. If it is still pink, you must cook it longer."

Annalisa nodded, soberly. "I understand."

"Now, while you're waiting for that, you may see if the potatoes are done."

Annalisa took a fork and poked it into a potato. "It is soft. The fork easily went through."

"Okay, so now you may drain and then mash the potatoes. Do you remember which utensil I use?"

"Yes, I used to call it the smasher. Sometimes Mom would let me mash potatoes. I remember she used to put butter and milk in them." Annalisa proceeded to finish this task.

"Sometimes I use only butter, other times butter with a little of the water they cooked in. Some use a little milk with butter, but you can decide which way you like best. Set it on the table when you're done. The table is set. I'll put the meat and vegetables on." She cut a strip of the simmering meat in half and showed Annalisa, who nodded. They both sat down, prayed, and ate.

"Thanks Aunt Catherine. There's so much to learn about cooking."

"Yes there is, my dear niece. Remember the more you do something the easier it becomes and the more you will learn. Your first meal is delicious, by the way."

"If my Mother could see me now, she would probably fall over in a dead faint. I never showed much interest in cooking before."

"She would not faint. She would instead be proud of you, just as I am. For a young girl who's had your experiences in the last month and a half, you've done extraordinarily well and adapted well," said Aunt Catherine.

"We need to clean up this kitchen, and I have homework to do for school tomorrow."

Annalisa began clearing the table and putting things away. After she had the table cleared, Aunt Catherine said, "I'll do the rest. You may get started on your homework."

"Thanks again, Aunt Catherine." They gave each other a big hug. An hour later, Annalisa heard the phone ring. Thinking it was for her, she went to the door so she'd hear if Aunt Catherine summoned her.

"Why, hello Zeke," she heard her aunt say in a happy voice.

Annalisa quietly closed the door, smiling to herself. The last two Sundays, she had noticed that Zeke waited for them on the front steps, smiled and tipped his hat. The previous Sunday, he and Aunt Catherine had walked down the steps together and visited for a whole five minutes. At the potluck that noon, he was near the door when they came in. When he smiled at Aunt Catherine, she showed him what she'd brought. Annalisa noticed later that his plate was heaped with her hot dish, and that he took several of her cookies for dessert. She even thought she saw him wave a cookie at Aunt Catherine and say, "Hmmmm."

Annalisa giggled to herself and finished her homework.

23

Plans for Thanksgiving

Next morning after the phone call, when she came to breakfast, Annalisa grinned. "Good mo-o-rning, Aunt Catherine" she said. "Did you enjoy your phone conversation last night?"

"Were you eavesdropping on me?" Catherine shook a finger at her with a stern look.

But Annalisa knew there was a twinkle behind it. "No, I didn't drop any eaves."

Catherine burst out laughing. She playfully snapped the dish towel at her.

"I opened the door, thinking you'd call me. But when I heard you say "Hello-o Zeke" in such a friendly voice, I closed it. So I didn't hear anything else."

"Well, it wouldn't have hurt anything. I'm not trying to hide anything from you. Sit down to breakfast now."

"You like him, huh?"

"Yes, he's a very nice man."

Annalisa folded her hands. "Let me ask the blessing this morning."

"Go ahead."

"Thank you, Father, for this food and that Aunt Catherine takes such good care of me. Thank you that she has Zeke for a friend so she doesn't have to be so lonely. Please bless their relationship. Thank you again. Amen."

"Umm. This quiche tastes delicious. Were you just so happy you had to make something special to celebrate?"

"Silly. Yes, I made it because I'm happy that I get to share my life with my beloved niece. And yes, I am happy to have a new friend in Zeke. He asked me to have dinner with him sometime."

"Good. What did you say?"

"I told him I would sometime, but that I'd have to think about when."

"And did he answer, 'Hmm?' Annalisa giggled.

Catherine laughed again and shook her head. After a few bites, she looked up. "Do you know it is only about three weeks till Thanksgiving Day?"

"Already?"

"Yes. I remember so many happy celebrations with you and your parents. It won't be the same with them gone."

They both ate silently a few minutes.

"Maybe—"Annalisa spoke softly, as if unsure—"We could invite Zeke over for dinner. Does he have any family, now that his sister has died?"

"No. The rest of his family had died years earlier." Catherine looked tentatively at Annalisa. "He did ask last night if he could take you and I out to *Jennies' Home Cooking,* over in the next town, for Thanksgiving Dinner."

"How about if we give him some *real* home cooking here? He obviously loves your cooking already. Then I could help you and learn how to fix turkey and stuffing or dressing, and green bean casserole and sweet potato casserole and pumpkin pie and..."

Catherine laughed. "I'm delighted to see the happy look that has come over your face. Is this really what you would like to do?"

Annalisa nodded, then drank her orange juice. "Look at the time! I better hurry to school.

Catherine nodded and hugged her goodbye. Todd and Travis arrived to give Annalisa a ride in their yellow Jeep. After school, she rode home with them again.

"Thanks a lot, guys." Annalisa jumped out and waved, then ran into the house.

I need to hurry to get all this homework done before supper, since I have youth group tonight. Oh good, I see Aunt Catherine has a casserole all prepared to put in the oven as soon as she gets home at 5.

She did her vocab first, then got busy on history. She read the chapter in her book, taking notes on what she read. Next she worked the problems in her math assignment. After rereading the section in her math text book, she worked the problems being careful not to make any foolish errors. She double-checked to see if she did it correctly. *There, that's done. Now the fun part.* Her English assignment was to read a chapter in the novel, "A Tale of Two Cities." She heard Catherine come in and stick the casserole in the oven, then come and peek in her door.

"Hi, Aunt Catherine. I have only one assignment left." She waved.

Aunt Catherine smiled and waved back, then went back downstairs.

Annalisa read the chapter with interest, then summarized what she had read and wrote a list of questions about things she was not sure of. She closed her book and notebook just in time for the call to supper.

As they ate, each talked about the day. Catherine had called Zeke at lunchtime and invited him to their house for Thanksgiving. He accepted with delight. "At least, it seemed like delight, as much as I could tell from a man of few words."

"Hmm! Delighted, mon Cherie." Annalisa giggled.

Catherine smiled. "Would you like to invite some friends, also?"

"Not for dinner, because their families will be having company I think. But maybe I could ask them to come for dessert and hot cider later on?"

"Yes, that will be fine. Go ahead and make plans with them. Who would you ask?"

"Mary Lou, maybe a couple other girls from youth group, Todd and Travis."

"You're getting to be quite close friends with those two young men, aren't you?

"Yes, they are very good to me."

"I just hope you don't get serious too soon. You still have high school to finish and then I hope you go on to college."

"Oh no, Aunt Catherine. They are not boyfriends, they're just friends. You don't need to worry. I intend to go to college right here at Pere Marquette University. I'll stay at home so you don't become lonely, and that will save on expenses. I'll only have to pay for tuition, books, and those things. Does that sound like a plan?"

"That sounds like a wonderful plan, my dear niece," said Catherine.

"I would not want you to cry yourself to sleep at night out of loneliness," said Annalisa with a smile and a twinkle in her eye. Of course, by then, you might be married to Zeke."

"Young lady, you watch your mouth!" Catherine threw a cloth napkin at her. "Of all the cheekiness! What are young girls coming to these days?"

Annalisa dissolved in laughter. "The same thing you were coming to. I remember Dad's stories of how you teased him and Grandpa and Grandma."

"Yes, we had a lot of fun together. I gave them baloney and they in turn gave it back to me. We laughed a lot together, just as you and I do."

They turned to the serious business of eating and discussing the menu for Thanksgiving Day. "Maybe, after dinner, we could all three play some games?" Annalisa said in a small voice. She remembered playing table games with her mom and dad. What fun they had!

"I'm sure we could do something fun like that. We'll have to show him our table games and see what he's interested in."

"He's probably interested in watching football, like most men."

When she was back in her room after youth group that evening, Annalisa made a list:

QUESTIONS I WANT TO ASK BRENDA:

1. *Brenda, will you be my friend?*
2. *Would you like to study together after school sometimes?*
3. *Do you read books for fun? What are your hobbies?*
4. *Here's a Bible I'd like to give you. May we look at some verses together?*

    a. *John 3:16 is a summary of the gospel in the entire Bible. "God so loved the world" means God loves you, Brenda.*
    b. *John 3:17 tells why Jesus came. "that the world through him might be saved."*

5. *Will you come to my church youth group with me on Wednesdays? The following Wednesday (a week before Thanksgiving) we are having a special Thanksgiving party. You'll see lots of students from school whom you already know. Aunt Catherine can give us rides to the church before and after.*

Feeling well-prepared with these notes, Annalisa changed into her night gown, brushed her teeth, said good night to her Aunt and crawled into bed. She prayed, summarizing her day, thanking God for His care and blessings, then closed her eyes and was soon sound asleep.

Witnessing

The next morning Annalisa awoke earlier than usual. She asked for God's blessing on her day, for his help with her classes, and that he would bless her meeting with Brenda.

She'd just finished her bath when her aunt knocked on the door. "Annalisa, is something wrong? Why are you up so early?"

"Wait a minute..." Soon Annalisa opened the door, clad in a big towel. "I'm sorry if I woke you. I rose early to pray about my meeting with Brenda. I want God to prepare her heart to hear the Bible Verses I want to show her. I also hope she'll go with me to youth group and that they'll accept her and welcome her."

"You've taken on quite a task, Annalisa. I'll also pray God will help you to be strong and courageous. Now what would you like for breakfast?"

"A bowl of courage, a big glass of inspiration, and two slices of fearlessness," said Annalisa, combing out her hair.

"Okay; would you like the courage in blueberry flavor and the inspiration in orange marmalade flavor?"

Annalisa laughed, then turned sober. "I'm scared, Aunt Catherine. I've not done this kind of thing before."

Aunt Catherine put a hand on her shoulder. "God will be with you today and especially while you are talking to Brenda. Try not to worry. Remember, I'll be praying for you today."

"The kids at youth group will be praying, also. They promised last night." Annalisa smiled and so did Catherine.

"I'll make eggs, bacon, and toast for you," said Aunt Catherine. "Choose a pretty dress to wear and put on a big smile. That will help you feel more confident."

"I wonder--, since Brenda has had a problem with jealousy, do you think wearing a pretty dress is the best idea?"

"That's a good point. I'm proud of you for being considerate of her feelings. Wear something comfortable, but not one that will make her jealous."

When Todd and Travis dropped Annalisa off at school, Travis said, "It's pretty cold today. We can give you a ride to the library for your meeting after school, since football is over."

"Thank you, that would be great!"

"Do you think Brenda would like a ride also?"

"I'll ask her. Thank you again for being so considerate and helpful to me."

"You're welcome. Bye." Todd said, smiling at her. They all headed to their own lockers.

Brenda came close when they'd turned the corner. "Annalisa, you have all the luck--- two handsome guys to give you rides to school and be your friends. I wish I had friends like you do."

"I'll help you, Brenda," said Annalisa. "Remember, you agreed to meet with me at the public library after school tonight?"

"Yes, I'll meet you there at 4:00 P.M."

"Todd and Travis will give me a ride. Travis asked if you would like a ride, also."

"Oh no. I'll just meet you there."

"Bye, Brenda," said Annalisa. "Have a good day."

The afternoon went well with no new assignments given, so Annalisa had a light load to take to the library. However, it was quite cold, so she was grateful for the ride in the yellow covered Jeep. She waited inside the front door of the library for five minutes before Brenda arrived, looking cold and out of breath. Finding a quiet corner, they sat down next to each other at a table and began talking.

"Brenda, as I said before, I would like to be your friend. Here's the Bible I promised to give you." Annalisa handed her a burgundy covered Bible she had bought with her own money. "May we look at some verses together?"

Brenda nodded, gently caressing the Bible.

"John 3:16 is a summary of the gospel in the entire Bible." Annalisa looked it up and pointed to the words. 'God so loved the world' means God loves you, too, Brenda." Brenda didn't say anything. She just sat there shaking her head slightly.

"John 3:17 tells why Jesus came. 'For God sent the Son into the world, not to condemn the world, but that the world might be saved through him.' I suggest you start reading the Bible here, in the Gospel of John. All four Gospels are about the life and death and resurrection of Jesus Christ, but from different perspectives. Pay special attention to what Jesus says and does."

Annalisa put one of her homemade crocheted cross bookmarks at the beginning of John, closed the Bible and handed it to Brenda. She took it and smiled tentatively.

"Brenda will you come to my church youth group meetings with me?"

"I'm not sure. I don't know them and would feel like a store window mannequin."

Annalisa grinned at the word picture of a mannequin on display. "I'll bet you do know several in our group. Mary Ann O'Reilly comes, as do Susan McCrea, Mary Lou, and Shari Taylor. There are many more girls too. Sam De Weerd, Bill Walters, and both Todd and Travis are members too."

"I somewhat know all of those," Brenda replied. "What do you do at those meetings?"

"We usually sing some gospel songs, have a Bible lesson, pray, have a snack and afterwards the boys talk with boys and the girls talk about girl things."

"Well, I'm familiar with some of those boring 300-year-old hymns, but since most of my clothing comes from the second hand stores uptown, I don't think I'd fit in. Count me out."

"Are you afraid someone will ridicule you for your clothing?" asked Annalisa, gently.

Brenda glared at her. "Yes. I'm sure all those kids don't have to shop at the Goodwill stores." She lowered her voice and turned her face away. "They will look down on me. That's partly why I don't have any friends."

Annalisa put her hand on her shoulder. She softly said, "Brenda...." Brenda turned back to look at Annalisa. Both had tears in their eyes. "I'd like to be one of your friends, and sometimes friends borrow clothes from each other. I'd like to get to know you better. May I?"

After a long couple minutes, Brenda nodded. "But I can't come this coming Wednesday. Mother has plans for me."

"A week from Wednesday the youth group is having a Thanksgiving party at the church. We will play games and have hot apple cider, donuts, and hot chocolate. Please say you'll come with me. It will be good for you to have fun with some nice young people. I think deep down inside you is a sweet girl wanting to rise to the surface. We'll be kind and respectful to you."

"Well, which church do you go to?" asked Brenda.

"I go to Gardenia Community Church. May my aunt and I pick you up?"

Brenda thought for a minute, then said, "Yes, you may. What should I wear?"

"Any of your school clothing would be just fine, but I'll bring a bag of clothes to school tomorrow which you are welcome to borrow if you wish. I'll be at your house at 5:45 pm that day. Give me your home address so I know where to find you."

"I live at 1063 Vine Avenue in a light blue house. Just knock on the front door when you arrive. I'll be ready to go."

Annalisa wrote that down, then looked at the clock. "Oh, I didn't realize the time was going by so fast! Here it is 5 pm and Aunt Catherine will be here soon to pick us up. She offered to give you a ride home, too." The girls put on their coats, gathered their belongings and went to the door just as she drove up.

When they got to Brenda's house, Brenda said, "See you at school next week, Annalisa."

"And I will give you girls a ride to the church the day of the party," said Aunt Catherine.

"Thanks, Aunt Catherine." Annalisa said, as they drove away. "I'm sure Todd and Travis would be glad to give us a ride, but I thought she might not be comfortable with that." She smiled at her aunt.

"I'm glad to do it, Dear. You may ask me, anytime."

The next week went by quickly. Annalisa attended the Grief Support Group for the sixth time on Tuesday. She felt much more comfortable than at first and joined freely in the sharing. She knew only a few at first, since most were juniors and seniors. But now she knew most of them. *I think this might be helpful to Brenda. I wonder...* Some said they had been stuck in anger for a long time, but now were beginning to accept what happened. Annalisa had talked about her reoccurring dreams, and they could relate. Then the dreams seemed to quit reoccurring.

Wednesday she went to youth group. Her friends rejoiced with her at the news about Brenda, and all promised again to pray for her.

Friday, she had another meeting at the library with Brenda. Brenda had been reading her Bible and asked some questions about it. She asked Annalisa to sign the "to... from" page, and seemed pleased with her "God bless you, Brenda" note. When they said goodbye, Brenda smiled at Annalisa, and said, "See you in school, and then Wednesday is the party."

Since Annalisa didn't have much homework that Friday evening, she had time to help her aunt make donuts for the youth group party. That way they'd have time to do a complete cleaning the next day. "We only need to bring a dozen, because others are also bringing some."

"Good. Then we can freeze some for Thanksgiving Day, too," Catherine said.

"Yes, and then Zeke will say "Ummm." Her aunt snapped a towel at her and chuckled.

"By the way, my dear niece, would you like to ride in a Zekemobile to church Sunday?"

"What—you mean the man of few words actually asked if you would like a ride?"

Aunt Catherine blushed and nodded.

"How did he do that? 'Ride Sunday, hmmm?'"

"Young lady, that's enough! You go clean your room now. And you'd better not embarrass him." Annalisa laughed, kissed her aunt, and ran up the stairs.

Aunt Catherine and Annalisa spent most of Saturday cleaning house. "Now that I have a job," Catherine said, "there won't be much time in the evenings to get ready for Thanksgiving Dinner. We can bake one pie Monday and one Tuesday evening, then prepare much of the rest on Wednesday since we both get off at noon."

Sunday morning dawned sunny but very cold. Catherine and Annalisa appreciated getting into Zeke's warm car. When they marched into the church together to sit in Zeke's usual spot, whispers occurred throughout the church such as,

"I've never seen Zeke sit with a lady before!"

"I've never even seen him talk to a lady."

"Oh, yes, he's talked to her after church before."

He took them to a fast food place for lunch. Annalisa enjoyed seeing the way he looked at Aunt Catherine and seeing how happy she seemed. *I wonder how I can get him to talk to me on Thanksgiving Day. I'd like to ask him if he likes to play table games, but I don't dare.* Remembering past Thanksgivings made her feel lonesome and tears came to her eyes. Her family had always spent time on holidays playing games together and reading together or doing something together. It wouldn't be the same this Thanksgiving.

She jumped when Zeke lightly bumped her elbow. "Hey," he said with a slight smile. "Do you play table games?"

"Why—why yes. I love to," she stammered.

"Let's do it Thanksgiving Day after dinner. You choose."

"Okay, great," she said, with a big smile. Then it was time to go home. Annalisa found herself singing around the house that next hour or so. *Seems there's something about a man of few words,* she thought. *I don't blame Aunt Catherine for liking him.*

Chapter

25

The Party

"Are you ready for the party?" Aunt Catherine called.

"Yes, I'll be down in a couple minutes." Annalisa knelt by her bed. "Dear Jesus, you know I've invited Brenda to our church's youth group party. I think Brenda is a bit scared about it. She doesn't have any close friends and I'm not sure if she goes to church at all. Please help all the members of the youth group to treat her with kindness and respect. Help us to have a good time and glorify your name."

"I'm ready, Aunt Catherine. Please pray that all will go well."

"I will, Annalisa. I hope you both have a good time."

"I do, also."

Catherine drove her to Brenda's, and Annalisa went up to the door. She stood there a few minutes before knocking on the door because she heard beautiful piano music.

"*Someone is a very good piano player,* she thought. *I wonder who it is?*"

When she knocked, the piano player stopped abruptly. Brenda opened the door and stepped outside. "Did you just arrive?" asked Brenda.

"Yes," said Annalisa, "and I heard the most beautiful piano music. Were you playing?"

Brenda's face turned red. She dipped her head and answered, "Yes."

"Wow! I didn't know you were so talented. It sounded beautiful."

"Thank you, but please don't tell anyone you heard me playing. Promise me." Brenda stopped walking and looked at Annalisa.

"Why...? All right, I promise I won't tell anyone I heard you play." They got into the car.

"Hello, Miss Schuiteman."

"Hello, Brenda. Please call me Catherine." They drove the six blocks to church.

"Thanks, Aunt Catherine. We'll ride home with someone from the group."

"Yes, thanks from me, too," Brenda said, surprising Annalisa with her politeness.

"You are both welcome." She drove away as they entered the church.

"We're a little early. Brenda, would you like a tour of the church? I'll just put Aunt Catherine's donuts in the kitchen first." She showed Brenda the sanctuary where worship services were held, then the Sunday School rooms and pointed out the offices and restrooms. By the time the quick tour was over, several other members of the youth group had come plus two sets of parents who had volunteered to supervise the group.

Mary Ann, Susan, Mary Lou and Shari were talking together when Annalisa and Brenda came into the fellowship hall. As soon as they saw them, they smiled and came to greet them. "Hi Brenda and Annalisa. It's good to see you here."

"Are you all ready for some fun?" Mary Ann asked. My mom is in charge of games, and they should be a blast. "We're going to play..."

Just then her mother clapped to ask for attention. "Welcome, everybody. We parents hope you all have a lot of fun this evening. Your regular youth leaders had to go somewhere else, so we O'Reillys and Taylors are in charge. Let's pray to ask God to bless our time together." After they prayed, Mrs. O'Reilly said, "First of all, just in case there is someone who doesn't know someone else, let's all stand in a circle and tell our names and one thing about ourselves. Now, usually when I've been in a group that did this, people said their names so quickly and softly that not everyone could hear it. So please, speak slowly and distinctly."

I'm so glad she said this, thought Annalisa. *It should be helpful to Brenda.*

Some of them said silly things about themselves like, "I used to make water bombs out of paper towels and dropped them out of the bathroom window." But most said what grade in school they were in or what hobby they liked. Brenda just said, "I'm a sophomore." Annalisa said, "I'm a sophomore, also, and I like English best of my subjects because I like to read and write." Some of the boys groaned.

"All right, now it's time for our first game: Pin the Wattle on the Turkey."

"Huh!"

"What's a wattle?"

"Every turkey has a wattle underneath it's beak. See this red, fleshy skin hanging down?"

Mrs. Taylor held up a large picture of a Turkey with a removable wattle. She took it off to show them, then pinned the turkey up on a bulletin board, while Mrs. O'Reilly finished explaining the rules of the game. Each one took a turn blindfolded to try to put the wattle in the right place on the turkey. The other adults would keep track of who was the closest, and the winner would get to do something special. Everyone laughed at the silly attempts.

Sam De Weerd won. "What's the 'something special' I get to do?"

Mr. Taylor told him, "You get to walk like a turkey." Everybody laughed.

"How do I do that?"

Mr. Taylor said, "Get down on your haunches like this, tucking your hands into your armpits. Lift your elbows up and down as you walk this way." He demonstrated and then stood up. "And you have to gobble while doing it."

Sam De Weerd not only complied with the instructions, but really got into it until everyone was laughing so hard tears ran down their cheeks. He had remarkable balance and continued for several minutes. When he finally stood up, everyone clapped.

"Remarkable show, Sam. Thank you. Since you did so well, you get a candy bar." He gave him a large salted nut roll.

"Yea, my favorite kind --- Thanks!"

"Now it's time for another game," said Mrs. O'Reilly. "Would a couple of you strong fellows help me put up these long tables?" All the "strong fellows" volunteered. Soon they had plenty of chairs around the tables for all eighteen of the young people present. The adult volunteers passed out a sheet of brown construction paper for each, plus pens and previously cut out orange "tail feathers"— four for each, plus small red pieces. Then Mrs. O'Reilly spoke again, "Here are the instructions: Put your hand on the brown construction paper and trace your fingers..."

"We did that in kindergarten," Bill blurted out.

"Good. Then you've had experience. The thumb will be the head of the turkey and the tail feathers go on the fingers. Before you glue them on, I want you to write on each tail feather at least one thing you are thankful for. Then add the wattle to the turkey's head."

"Does that winner get to walk like a turkey, too?" asked Mary Lynn.

"Everyone wins on this one," said Mr. O'Reilly. It is always beneficial to give thanks."

When they had all finished, they each received a candy bar. Mrs. O'Reilly asked, "Is there anyone who would like to share something they wrote on their feathers, or something meaningful about this experience?"

"I am thankful my dad got a job this week," exclaimed Tom. "He'd been off work for a year, and it's been tough."

"Hey, I can relate to that," said Marcos. "Mine was off work last year. Since he got that job at the factory last January, it's been much easier for us. Tell him to apply there."

"I'm thankful my sister had a healthy baby. She is so cute," said Cindy.

"I'm thankful for all my friends here," said Annalisa. "It has helped a lot since my parents died to know that I have friends who care about me." She looked around and smiled at them all.

"Wow, this has been a good exercise," said Marlys. "It makes me realize I should be more thankful. God has blessed me and my family so much, and yet sometimes I grumble."

"Yes, that's what I feel, also," said Travis. "Here we are, blessed beyond measure simply by being in God's family through the death and resurrection of Jesus Christ, knowing that because he lives we also shall live eternally. That relationship also includes the peace of knowing we are forgiven, and the joy of knowing God is working for good in our lives. I am ashamed that I sometimes complain."

"Maybe we should sing a Thanksgiving song," said Daryl.

Mrs. Taylor went to the piano. "How about *Thanks to God for my Redeemer*? This was written by a young Swede who based it on a list he had made of many things to be thankful for."

Mary Lou, Betsy, and Margaret grabbed the hymnals off the piano and passed them around. They sang all three verses with enthusiasm.

When they'd finished the song, Mr. Taylor asked, "Is anyone hungry?"

Several cried "Yes!"

"You may get into two lines to help yourselves to donuts, and cider or hot chocolate. There should be plenty for each of you to have two or three donuts."

As people ate, they stood around or sat in twos or threes visiting. Brenda and Annalisa sat at the end of one table. "I'm glad I came," Brenda said. "This has been fun."

"I hope you will keep coming, Brenda," said Annalisa.

Betsy sat down beside Brenda with her donut and hot chocolate. "We're so glad you came, Brenda. I've seen you some at school, but never had the chance to get acquainted, since we're usually hurrying to the next class." Shari nodded her agreement. Brenda started visiting with them, while Mary Lou sat down at the other side of Annalisa, who had been her best friend since grade school. They told each other their Thanksgiving plans.

After letting the group visit for several minutes, pleased that everyone seemed to have a good time, the adult volunteers told the group, "As most of you know, there won't be a meeting next Wednesday since it is the evening before Thanksgiving. We want to wish each of you a very happy Thanksgiving. Your regular leaders will expect to see you all the following week. Now we want to close this party with one more activity. We'd like each of you to pair up with one other person and each tell the other person one thing you are thankful for about that person."

Quickly, each person found someone to pair up with. Brenda looked at Annalisa as if she didn't know what to do. Annalisa quickly grabbed her hand and they walked to a corner of the room. The adults looked around, making sure each one had a partner, then they did the exercise with their own partners.

"Brenda, I am thankful that you are a person who keeps her promises. It meant a lot to me tonight that you kept your promise to come with me. I am beginning to see that wonderful person inside of you rising to the surface." Brenda looked shy and even blushed a little.

"Annalisa, I am thankful you asked me to be your friend and to come to this party. You are such a loving person. I hope I can grow to be more like you."

Soon, Todd came over and asked if they would like a ride home. "Yes, we would, Todd. Thank you," Annalisa said. While he went to see if Travis was ready she said to Brenda, "Aunt Catherine said I could have a few friends over for dessert and apple cider Thanksgiving evening. Would you like to come?"

"Thank you, but I'll be going out of town with my mother. She has that day off so has made plans for us." She grimaced. "But I do want to come to youth group again."

"Good. We'll plan on that. Do you want to study together at the library sometime?"

"Maybe next week. I better focus on more piano practice this week. Mom wants me to play for some people on Thanksgiving Day." Annalisa could see pain in her eyes.

"We're ready if you are," said Todd and Travis. Brenda and Annalisa quickly put on their coats and left with them after saying "Goodbye" and "Happy Thanksgiving" to others.

At Brenda's house, Annalisa remarked, "The house is all dark. Isn't your mother home?"

"No, she worked extra hours today. She won't be home until later. Bye. Thanks for the ride." Brenda quickly got out of the car.

"I wonder if her mother knew..."

"I doubt it," said Todd.

They were soon at Annalisa's house. Before she got out, she told them, "Aunt Catherine said I could have a few friends over for dessert and apple cider Thanksgiving evening. Would you like to come?"

"Sure, if our parents don't mind," Travis answered. "All the relatives will be there for dinner at 1pm."

"I was thinking like 6 or 7 pm."

"That should be all right. Sounds like fun. Is Brenda coming?"

"No, she has to go somewhere with her Mom, but I'll ask some other friends." Todd opened the door for her. "Thank you, kind Sir. Bye, both of you and thanks for the ride."

Chapter

26

Thanksgiving Day

Annalisa hurried to finish her homework after school Monday so she could help Aunt Catherine bake cookies and a mince meat pie. They made ginger snaps, molasses crinkles and almond bars. Tuesday evening they baked an apple pie, pumpkin pies, and banana bread. Wednesday both came home at noon, had lunch together and prepared the turkey for stuffing.

"I always like to wash it thoroughly, even though it looks clean from the store," Aunt Catherine explained. "Sometimes the inside doesn't seem cleaned out well enough for my liking. That's why I scrape this out with my fingers and then rinse it thoroughly."

"Do you use these parts?" Annalisa held up the neck and giblets.

"I don't like the liver. I used to give that to a friend who had a cat. But I do cook the heart, gizzard, and neck in the forward cavity after I stuff it. The meat on the neck is one of my favorites."

"How do we make the stuffing?" Annalisa asked.

"You may start that while I finish cleaning this turkey. First put two cubes of butter in this large kettle to melt on low. Then cut up these six stalks of celery (which I've already washed) and this large onion and add to the melted butter. Sprinkle poultry seasoning all over it, add a tablespoon of sage, half tablespoon salt and a teaspoon of pepper. Then add this bag of croutons and mix it all together. Then we'll add a little hot water to moisten it so it will stick together." Catherine showed her where to put the stuffing into both ends of the turkey and sew the one end shut. The back end was held shut by a device on the legs which, when the tail was stuffed between them, held the cavity shut. The neck was placed just inside the opening. "I know this is an old-fashioned method," Catherine said. "Nowadays many people put the stuffing into a crock pot to cook instead of into the turkey. But this is how my mother did it, and this is how I like to do it. Now we will put the bird in the refrigerator until early in the morning when I will put it in the oven. It will need to roast at 325 degrees for about six hours."

By the time they cleaned up the kitchen, Aunt Catherine looked very tired. "Would you like a nap, Annalisa? Because I sure would. We can peel the potatoes after supper, then fix the other dishes in the morning." By 9 pm, everything was ready to put in the oven or microwave the next day, and since they'd cleaned thoroughly on Saturday, the house was quickly readied, also.

By Thanksgiving morning, both women were well-rested and excited for the day. Zeke picked them up for church and, after bringing them home afterward, stayed for the day. "Hmmm," Zeke said with every new thing he tasted and finally, "Catherine, this was delicious!"

Annalisa dropped her fork, making a clattering noise on her plate. He turned to her and asked, "Now, Annalisa, what game have you chosen for us to play?"

Annalisa recovered from her surprise and brought out the "Ungame" as Catherine started putting the leftover food away. "Have you ever played this?" she asked.

"No, how do we do it?"

"Well, this is my version. Each player picks a card to ask another person a question. If you don't like the card, you can keep picking another until you find a question you want to ask someone. You say who the question is for, then read it and that person answers it. It's a communication game, so helps people get better acquainted... no winners or losers, but it's fun."

"Okay, let's play it." Zeke grabbed a card, stared at it, then put it back and took another. "Annalisa, describe your favorite minister."

"Oh that's easy. Pastor Jim Brady. He is sympathetic and kind, preaches good sermons, and has a good sense of humor. He's about 5'10" and has thinning brown hair, is a tiny bit chubby, but has a pleasant look about him. Your turn, Aunt Catherine."

She sat down and picked a card. "Zeke, 'What is your definition of a Christian'?"

"One who believes Jesus is the Son of God who came to rescue us, and who lets him be boss," Zeke answered.

"Now it's my turn," Annalisa said. "Both of you tell me, 'What character in the Bible do you relate to?'" She looked at Zeke expectantly.

Zeke's eyes crinkled as he smiled and answered, "Andrew, a disciple of Jesus who brought people to him."

"I suppose Martha would be the one I most relate to," said Catherine. "I've always been particular about housework and fussed a lot about cooking. Yet, my sister-in-law was the one who really spent a lot of time listening to Jesus. Since she died, I feel my own personal relationship with Jesus has become more authentic and deeper, as I think about her witness."

Annalisa thought about her mother listening to Jesus. *If she hadn't listened so well, maybe she'd still be alive.* But with the next breath, she realized *This is one of the things I liked best about my mom. She loved Jesus and obeyed him explicitly... She was a great mom because of it. I wouldn't want her to have been any different.*

"Catherine, 'Thank God for three things'." Zeke smiled at Catherine with that soft look.

"Why, I'm thankful my brother and sister-in-law knew the Lord so I can be sure they are in Heaven. I'm thankful to have the privilege of living with and caring for my niece here. I'm thankful we three can have this time together." She directed a similar soft look at Zeke.

"Annalisa, what is your favorite memory of Thanksgiving?" asked Catherine.

"You and I, Mom and Dad, Grandpa and Grandma were all here together. Everyone was happy and telling what they were thankful for, and telling stories and playing games.

It felt so cozy and secure. Kind of like it feels now, except there's someone missing." Tears began to fill her eyes. "And then we all sang together, 'Thanks to God For My Redeemer.'"

"Would you like to sing it now, Annalisa?" The young girl nodded. Catherine started and Zeke and Annalisa sang with her. They knew nearly every word, so didn't need a book. Annalisa noticed Zeke knew it quite well, also. When they got to the part "Thanks for pain, and thanks for pleasure" in the second verse, the eyes of all three filled with tears. By the third verse, when they sang about joy, sorrow, heavenly peace and hope, tears were running down all their cheeks.

"Amen" exclaimed Zeke. They all wiped their eyes.

"Zeke, I have another question for you," said Annalisa.

"Okay, shoot."

"Tell me about your life." *I wonder how a man of few words will answer this one.*

Zeke thought quietly about that until they thought he might not answer. "Hmmmmm. Well, I was born the son of a carpenter. He built the cradle I slept in as well as all the furniture in our house. He was trying to be a farmer, but that didn't go so well. So he moved his wood-working into a vacant building, hired someone to run the farm, and began building furniture full-time when I was about five. He called the shop *Vander Broek Carpenter Shop*. As the years went by, I would go there after school and help him for a couple hours every day. I learned a lot from him about carpentry work, but it didn't get into my blood like it did his. Since he was so busy there, he didn't have time to fix things at home. So I worked with the hired farmer to do repairs around the place. He taught me a lot, too, and I seemed to have a natural knack for it. Pa liked to build new things, but I liked to fix things that were broken down. After a couple years in the army, I developed Post Traumatic Stress Syndrome. I couldn't cope with life for awhile. I felt like I was broken down—like I needed fixing. That's when I met the Lord Jesus. He healed me. That's when I was reborn as the son of a Carpenter. After that, Mom and Dad helped me start my own shop called *Vander Broek Fixit Shop* and I began doing handyman jobs all over the area. I had one sister, Phyllis, who had a seamstress shop in town until she died in that plane crash. She was married for several years, until her husband died in a hunting accident five years ago. They had no children. Our parents died of illness three years ago."

Zeke stopped and looked at Catherine and Annalisa. "Any questions?"

I can't believe he had that many words in him! Annalisa thought. "Yes, Zeke. Haven't you ever been married?"

"No."

"Why not?"

"I was rather shy around women, and after the army I felt too depressed to relate to anyone. When I got well, I just didn't see the type of woman I would want to marry..." he looked briefly at Catherine...

Until now? thought Annalisa, hiding a smirk.

"I'm tired of talking now. How about if we play train dominoes instead?" Zeke asked

"That sounds like a good idea," said Catherine. "Annalisa, would you help me clear the table? Then we will have room for the dominoes." The next couple of hours they played that with a lot of jocularity.

When the game was finished, Zeke stood up and stretched."Would you ladies like to go for a little walk? It's about 35° degrees out there."

"Too cold for me," said Annalisa. "Besides, I want to get things ready for when my friends come over. You two go ahead."

By the time they returned, Annalisa had set out the desserts: pumpkin pie, apple pie, mince meat pie, ginger cookies, chocolate chip cookies, molasses crinkles, almond bars, banana bread and hot apple cider. Zeke's eyes almost popped out of his head when he saw it all.

The doorbell rang and Catherine went to answer it. "Happy Thanksgiving, Miss Schuiteman."

"Happy Thanksgiving to you, too, Todd and Travis. I don't believe I know your friend's name."

"This is Steve Schuller. He lives just up the street from us. They moved in just a week ago. I called Annalisa and she said it was okay to bring him."

"Sure, the more the merrier. Speaking of more, here come the girls." Amidst a flurry of introductions and greetings, Mary Lynn, Mary Lou, and Betsy joined the group.

Aunt Catherine asked Annalisa, "Would you and your friends like to sit around the dining room table? Or would you rather sit in the living room?"

"In the living room, please. There are tables in there to set their drinks on, or TV trays I can put up if they need them." Then we can enjoy the fireplace.

"That will be fine," Catherine said. She and Zeke ate their dessert at the table while the young people laughed and joked and talked in the living room. One time when Annalisa went to the kitchen to get some more cookies and cider, she overheard the adults talking at the table:

"I think this is the nicest Thanksgiving Day I've ever had, Catherine. Thank you."

Catherine smiled. "You're welcome, Zeke. I have enjoyed it, also." He put his hand over hers on the table, and she didn't take it away.

"Bye everyone" Annalisa called again as the last of her friends were out the door a couple hours later. Soon Zeke left, also.

While they were doing dishes, Catherine asked "How was your party?"

"Oh, it was fun, Aunt Catherine. Thanks for letting me have them over."

"There sure was a lot of laughing going on! What was so funny?"

"Todd had brought a little book called *Teen Book of Hilarity* and was reading from it. There were some extremely funny jokes in there. Then the new guy—Steve, started mimicking different accents and certain comedians. Then we played a little game where one person starts a story but says only one sentence or one paragraph, and each person adds to it."

"I'm glad you had fun, Dear." Catherine hugged her and kissed her on the cheek."

The rest of the holiday weekend, Annalisa and her aunt spent a lot of time relaxing by the fireplace, reading or watching TV movies together, and doing little things around the house they didn't usually have time to do. Soon it was time to go back to school and work.

Brenda & Annalisa at Library

"This afternoon, Aunt Catherine, I plan to go to the library with Brenda," Annalisa announced the Monday after Thanksgiving. "Would you mind dropping by there on your way home from work and give us a ride?"

"I would be glad to. It might be a little later than five, however, since it's the first day back after four days off. I'm not sure how busy we'll be. I'll text you when I know."

"Thank you. We'll just wait inside until you come. Or if you're going to be quite late, should we walk?"

"We'll see. I'll let you know."

Brenda and Annalisa walked to the library after school. The temperature had warmed up to fifty, so it wasn't bad at all. "Would you explain why you want to keep such talent a secret?" Annalisa asked, referring to Brenda's request about not telling about her piano playing.

Brenda shifted her backpack. After a moment she answered, "My mother wanted to be a concert pianist when she was a young girl. A neighbor gave her lessons and she practiced hard, but she couldn't afford to go to college, much less any fancy music school, so she couldn't become skilled enough to do it. So now she thinks I have to fulfill her dream. She thinks I can earn a music scholarship big enough to pay for college, if I practice hard enough. But I don't want to be a concert pianist." Brenda looked dejected.

"Brenda, that is sad. It is understandable that you would want to make your own choices.

What do you want to do with your life?" asked Annalisa.

"I wanted to become a Medical Doctor, but since I had to practice piano all the time instead of do homework, my grades are probably not good enough to become a doctor. All I learned is music. I had to study piano and practice since I was five years old. Now I'm sixteen and still taking lessons. It's always lessons. My mother even has a school of music chosen for me, The Eastman School of Music in Rochester, New York. She has sent tapes of my piano playing and they think I am skilled enough to be admitted. I, however, do not want to go to school there." Brenda clenched her teeth and tightened her fists. Tears came.

Annalisa put her arm around Brenda and patted her shoulder. "Brenda, I won't tell anyone of your musical talent if you don't want me to, although I still don't think it is something you need to hide. May I make a suggestion to you?"

"What do you suggest?" asked Brenda.

"My suggestion is that you see a counselor about this problem with your mother."

"I've been talking with Mrs. Hoffman some."

"Good." By then, they had reached the library. They found their favorite private spot and took off their coats. They both worked on homework for awhile.

Annalisa closed her book. "What is required to become a concert pianist?" she asked.

"Why? Are you thinking of becoming a concert pianist?" asked Brenda.

"No, I'm just wondering what your mother expects of you. But I am still thinking of what I want to do with my life. I'm not looking for a lot of money, just what God wants me to be."

"What God wants you to be?" Brenda's eyes opened wide. "You hear God speak to you?"

"Not in an audible voice, but by reading the Bible and praying, sometimes I sense in my mind or heart a quiet voice speaking to me. Or the voice could be in a sermon, an article, a conversation with a missionary, or maybe a friend. As long as I'm open to God and following him, I believe he'll let me know his will for my life. When I follow his will, I will be successful and happy."

Brenda looked dubious. "Do you mean God will make you rich and famous?"

"No, that's not what I mean. To me, success means God is pleased with me. And if He's pleased with me, I'm happy."

Brenda looked at her for a long moment as if she were from another planet.

"Well, since you asked," Brenda said in a reciting voice, "the requirements to become a concert pianist are:

First of all one needs a solid foundation of many years of piano lessons to learn how to read and play very difficult music. Then one needs to practice as much as possible, preferably eight hours a day. A concert pianist must have dedication, passion, a thorough knowledge of music theory, and a love for music. Such a person would need to study music and all the technical aspects of the piano. Pianists must start at a young age playing for audiences, family, and others who will give an honest critique of their performance so they become comfortable playing the piano in front of people. Some say a pianist needs to create a gimmick; a style of playing that is unique to that pianist only. The aspiring pianist must play in competitions and be prepared to receive criticisms but not let negative criticism discourage her (or him). Also, he or she must take lessons from the best teachers and enroll in the best schools."

"Wow, Brenda, that sounds like all you would need to do is music. There wouldn't be time for anything else. Almost like you would eat, sleep, and do nothing but music. When do you get to be a child and do childish things, or a teenager, and go to ball games, have a slumber party, or go on a date while in high school?"

Brenda slumped in discouragement. "That's just it. It seems like all you do is music."

The next day Brenda went to visit the school counselor before school.

"Hello Brenda," Mrs. Hoffman said. "I've seen you and Annalisa together. Are you getting along better now?"

"Yes. We are becoming friends. She convinced me she wanted to, which I found hard to believe. She invited me to their church youth group Thanksgiving party and loaned me nice clothes to wear. It was the most fun I've had in a long, long time."

"That's nice. It's wonderful to have a friend you can do things with."

"We were talking yesterday, and she suggested I talk with you about my problem with my mother. She didn't know I've already talked with you some."

"I remember you were upset that your mother insists you practice four hours a day, and you feel she's forcing you into a career you don't want."

"That's just it. Mother keeps telling me what I must do, and I haven't been allowed a voice in the matter. I'm expected to live my life according to what she wants, not what I would like. I can't take it anymore, and now I find myself sneaking out and scared she will find out."

"You mean she didn't know you had gone to the youth group party?"

"That's right. She was at work and I knew she wouldn't be home until later. It seemed like such a good thing to do, but now I feel guilty that I did something without her permission."

Mrs. Hoffman promised again that she and the principal would have a talk with her mother. "But as long as you are under eighteen, she has the legal right to make the rules for you. I suggest you talk with her about what you'd like to do and get her permission."

Brenda knew Mrs. Hoffman was right. *But she doesn't realize how difficult it is for me to talk with my mother, especially about things we disagree about.*

She tried to explain her feelings that evening to her mother, just as they were finishing supper. "Mother, there's this group of teenagers who meet together one evening a week. I would like to join them."

"You are already so busy with homework you don't have time to practice as much as you should. You don't have time to join a group. Remember a concert pianist in-the-making must stay focused. Now go to the piano and focus."

"But Mother, I need friends!"

"No you don't. You need to practice. Now get busy."

The next day, Annalisa talked Brenda into going with her at noon hour to the Grief Support Group meeting. "I brought an extra sandwich and pudding, in case you would agree."

Brenda agreed.

After they were all seated and eating their lunches, Mrs. Hoffman introduced Brenda and told her a little about the members of the group. "Would you like to tell us how long it is since your loss, Brenda?"

Brenda looked scared at first. She blurted out, "My Dad died over three years ago."

Annalisa's heart went out to her. She knew it would be harder for her to tell the rest of the story. The others came up to Brenda to introduce themselves and many said compassionate words.

Travis addressed the group. "We have all had different experiences with our grief. Some of us were able to talk about it right away with loved ones, while others have had to bear the pain alone for years. The main purpose of this group is to give grievers a comfortable setting in which to talk, because talking about your grief will help you heal. Can anyone vouch for this?"

"Yes, I can," said an older boy Annalisa didn't know well. "I was grieving alone for several months about my brother, because I thought 'real men don't cry.' Finally, my aunt took me on an all-day outing so she could talk with me. She convinced me it is all right and proper and even beneficial to cry when a loved one dies. She talked about her memories of my brother and how much she missed him, and that got me to talking until I thought I'd never stop. I felt a lot better after that. I called her up after that whenever I needed to talk."

Travis nodded. "Besides sadness, many of us have also had confusing emotions such as guilt, confusion, fear, disorientation, even relief. This is normal. Remember 'feelings are neither good nor bad, they just are.' We need to accept our emotions and ourselves as we are."

Annalisa spoke up. "I felt angry at God because I couldn't understand why he would allow my parents to be killed while they were trying to serve Him on a mission trip. I felt like I couldn't trust him anymore. But I have a very loving aunt to talk with, plus the support of my church and youth group and other friends. I realized later that God does not cause evil to happen. Evil is simply part of this world we live in. But God does use evil for good."

Annalisa's voice cracked. She quit talking and got out her handkerchief.

Mrs. Hoffman broke the silence. "It's normal to keep asking 'why? Why did my loved one die? If God is so all-powerful, why did he allow this to happen?' We may never know the answers to why God does or doesn't do certain things. But we can be reassured that he is holy and righteous, he knows what he is doing, and he is love. When I lost my child, many years ago, I went through a long period of grief and of questioning God. One book that helped me deal with the questions is one by Anne Graham Lotz, _Why?Trusting God When I Don't Understand._ I have copies of both the paperback and the audio book which you may borrow."

Travis looked around. "Would anyone else like to share something that helped?"

Annalisa slowly raised her hand a few inches. When he nodded to her, she said, "I decided I had a choice. I could be bitter, or I could return to trusting God. When I was angry at God, I didn't like myself. After all, he's God, not me. So he must be right. I decided to forgive him and trust him. That makes me feel happier and I know that honors my parents more, too."

Several others shared their feelings also, until the noon hour was over.

As the two girls left the meeting, Brenda turned to Annalisa. "Wow! I never heard people spill their guts like that before!"

Annalisa smiled at the expression. "It does seem unusual for people to be so open about their feelings. But it gives a feeling of release and of community, knowing others understand."

They hurried to class as Annalisa asked, "Shall we pick you up for youth group tomorrow?

Brenda hesitated. Just as the bell rang, she said, "Yes.

Chapter

28

Youth Group Anyway

Aunt Catherine gave Annalisa and Brenda a ride to youth group Wednesday evening. The girls rushed into the church quickly. "Brr! It's cold outside!" said Annalisa.

Brenda agreed, but she was more preoccupied by the heat she would meet when she returned home. Her mother would be home in a half hour, and find her gone.

"Hi Amber. We missed you at the party," Annalisa said.

"We were out of town all week. You should see how much makeup homework I have!"

Amber rolled her eyes. "It was fun, though. We went to Disney World again."

"I'd like you to meet Brenda," Annalisa continued. "She goes to the same school I do, so you probably don't know her." She explained to Brenda, "Amber goes to the Christian School." Brenda tried to smile at Amber. It did feel good to have someone introducing her as if she were important. If only she could keep coming.

"Hi girls." A girl with long blonde hair said to Brenda, "In case you forgot, I'm Cindy, and this is Marlys. We're so glad you could join us again."

"We go to the same school as Amber," Marlys said.

Then a group of boys came up. "Hi, Annalisa and Brenda." *I don't remember who these are. There are too many...* Brenda didn't know what to say.

Annalisa came to her rescue by reminding her, pointing to each one, "This is Tom, this one Daryl, and this is Bill."

"Welcome back to our group. We've seen you at school, too."

An older, jolly-looking couple also came to Brenda and told her, "We are the adult sponsors of this group of fine young people. My name is Carrie and this is my husband Terry."

"You rhyme," observed Brenda, with a smile. Carrie smiled and patted her shoulder.

"Yes, we do. I understand you were here at the party, so you've met most of these."

"Feel free to visit until we start," added Terry with a smile. "We will have a Bible story about Gideon tonight. Then some snacks and hot chocolate after the lesson. Enjoy yourself."

When everyone had arrived, Terry said, "Gather around, guys and girls. Sit anywhere you like, the closer to me the better. Please open your Bibles to Judges, chapter 6, and I will tell you the story of Gideon...the short form."

"Now, Israel had wandered away from God. Verse 1 says 'they did evil in the eyes of the Lord.' (In the Living Bible, it says they were worshiping other gods. This is a great evil to God.) So God allowed the Midianites to overrun Israel and make their lives miserable by stealing their food and ruining their crops. The children of Israel were starving and discouraged. So they cried out to God to save them. Terry asked, "If you were God, what would you do?"

"Let them starve," said Daryl.

Cindy commented, "Yes, they deserve whatever happens. If they had stayed close to God and been faithful to him, they wouldn't have had the problem."

"But if God was their Father," Betsy offered, "wouldn't he protect them?"

Nick looked at Betsy, "How could he protect them if they wouldn't obey him?"

Terry nodded, "That's just it. He had to find someone who would obey him before he could help the people who wouldn't obey. Israel did deserve everything that was happening to them. Those were the consequences of their own disobedience. But God still loved them. He heard their cries and sent an angel to talk to Gideon. Now, why Gideon?"

Various guesses were offered. One said, "God must have known he would obey."

Terry continued. "While Gideon was threshing wheat (in a wine press to hide it from the Midianites), the angel came to Gideon and said, 'The Lord is with you, you mighty man of valor,' (this means mighty warrior)."

"But sir, said Gideon, if the Lord is with us, why has all of this happened to us?"

"Then the Lord told Gideon he was sending him to save Israel out of Midian's hand.

"Now, Gideon didn't feel like a 'mighty man of valor.' See verse 15. He felt like a weakling. But the Lord promised to be with him. You can read the next verses to see how God convinced him it was really the Lord speaking and that he understood the Lord correctly. Once convinced, he obeyed in drastic ways. He tore down his father's altar to Baal and cut down the Asherah pole, built a proper altar to the Lord, and offered a burnt offering using his father's bull.

"The next morning the town was in an uproar because Baal's altar was destroyed.

"But Gideon's father, Joash, calmly said, "Does Baal need your help? What kind of a wimpy God is he if he needs the likes of you to help him? If he is any kind of a god, let him do his own defending and destroy the one who broke his altar in pieces."

"Jim find Judges 6:33-40 and summarize it for us, please."

"I'll be glad to, sir. The Midian army was joined by others against Israel. The Spirit of the Lord came upon Gideon and he blew a trumpet to call the fighting forces to come. Then Gideon must have got scared. He asked God for proof that he would save Israel through him. He said, 'I'll place a wool fleece on the threshing floor tonight. If in the morning the fleece is wet and the floor is dry, I will know that you will save Israel by my hand.' The next morning Gideon took the wool fleece and wrung out a full bowl of water, but the ground was dry. Then he asked God to do the opposite. And he did."

"Thank you for summarizing that passage, Jim," Terry said. Any questions so far?"

Shari Taylor raised her hand. "Terry, I've heard about people 'laying out a fleece,' but I've never really understood what it means and if it is good or bad."

"That's a good question, Shari. I'm not sure I can answer it satisfactorily. In Gideon's case, what do verses 36-37 say was his purpose for the test?"

"He wanted to be certain God was going to use him to save Israel."

"Yes, he wondered if he heard right. By doing what he asked, God gave him confidence for leading the army. I don't see any place where it says God was mad at him for asking. He just wanted to be double sure that he was doing the Lord's will. Then he confidently led the men out to fight the enemy."

"Mary Ann, please summarize Judges 7:1-7."

"Well, Gideon and his army gathered. The armies of Midian were camped north of them down in the valley. The Lord said to Gideon, 'There are too many of you. I can't let all of you fight the Midianites, for then the people of Israel will boast to me that they saved themselves by their own strength. Send home those who are afraid.' Only 10,000 remained who were willing to fight. God said, 'There are still too many. Bring them down to the spring and I'll show you which ones shall go with you and which ones shall not.' He ended up with only 300 and conquered the Midianites with these."

"What a strange way to choose a fighting group," said Henry.

"I know," said Terry, the group leader. "We need to realize that God has a purpose for everything He does.

Everything must fit into His plan. The difference in numbers would make any soldier tremble in his combat boots. However, with the numbers as they were, there could be no doubt that God was the deciding factor in the battle. This would build up the people's faith. "

Terry stood up to ask the group, "What is a message for us in this scripture?"

"We need to place our confidence in God, not in ourselves," said Todd.

"Check to make sure that what you think you hear God saying is really him," said Tricia.

"Obey God, even if it might make people mad at you," said Amber.

"These are all good answers," said Terry.

"Daryl, would you please summarize Judges 7:8-13?"

"During the night, with the Midianites camped in the valley just below, the Lord said to Gideon, 'Take your troops and attack the Midianites. I'll cause you to defeat them. But first go down to the camp with your servant, Purah, and listen to what they are saying. You will be greatly encouraged and be eager to attack.' So he took Purah and crept down through the darkness to the outposts of the enemy camp. The vast armies were crowded across the valley like locusts, or sand upon the seashore. Gideon crept up to one of the tents and heard one of the enemy soldiers say, 'I had this strange dream. There was this huge loaf of barley bread that tumbled down into our camp. It hit our tent and knocked it flat,' (7:13).

'The other soldiers replied, "your dream can mean only one thing. Gideon, the son of Joash, the Israelite, is going to come massacre all the allied forces of Midian.'

"That was a strange dream," said Daryl. "To think Gideon would choose that particular tent to crawl up to and hear about that dream."

"Yes," said Terry, "it shows that God was in control, doesn't it? When Gideon heard the dream and the interpretation, he worshiped God. Then he returned to his men and shouted, 'Get up, for the Lord is going to use you to conquer all the vast armies of Midian. '300 conquered with trumpets and clay jars with torches inside as they shouted, 'We fight for God and Gideon.'"

"That sounds like a strange battle plan," said Cindy.

"You're right, Cindy, but God was fighting for Israel that night," said Carrie.

"Let's pray to close the meeting. Father, we thank you for this story of Gideon as recorded in the Bible. Gideon answered your call to fight against evil and trusted you to help him win the battle against Midian and its allies. Help us to trust you as well in all things. Amen."

After a time of visiting and snacks, Brenda and Annalisa got a ride home with Todd and Travis. When they reached Brenda's house, they noticed lights were on this time. Travis jumped out to open Brenda's door. "Thank you," she said. "I really enjoyed it."

Annalisa thought Brenda seemed scared. "Let's pray for her," she said, as Brenda walked to the door. So they did, as they drove away

Anger Explodes

Brenda opened the door in fear and trepidation. She knew her mother had expected her to be home practicing all evening.

"Who was that man?"

Brenda jumped at the sudden, stern voice. She turned to see her mother standing in the dark living room at the nearest window.

"That was Annalisa's friend, Travis. He is like a big brother to her. He and his cousin Todd look out for her since her parents died. They both are like brothers to her."

"Just where have you been tonight?" demanded her mother, with her hands on her hips.

Brenda's eyes began to sting. "Mother, I went with Annalisa to a youth group meeting at her church. Lots of teens from school were there. We listened to an adult leader teach a Bible lesson, then had snacks and visited with each other.

"Why did you go to a church? We haven't gone to church since we moved here," She frowned. "I don't believe you!"

Tears began to flow down Brenda's cheeks. "Mother, I'm not lying. We used to attend church years ago. I miss that."

"You should have been at home practicing music by Chopin, Stravinsky, and Beethoven. How will you be a concert pianist if you don't practice several hours daily?" She demanded.

"Has the thought ever occurred to you, Mother, that maybe I would like to choose my own future instead of you doing it for me? I really do not want to be a concert pianist."

"What?" Brenda's mother gasped a huge breath and clutched her heart. She placed her hands on her hips again and shouted, "You *will* be a concert pianist. I've spent hundreds and thousands of dollars on lessons for you and you are an excellent pianist. This has been our dream all your life."

"I will not!" Brenda shouted. Then she fought to get her voice under control. It wouldn't do any good to shout. She took off her coat, then spoke in a more subdued, yet emphatic, voice. "This has been your dream, not mine," she replied.

Her mother stood with her hands on her hips, and her mouth open. "Well, I never thought I would hear such words from my daughter. Such ingratitude for all I've done for you."

Brenda's face was red with anger and with the effort to control herself. She took time to hang up her coat in the closet. In a few moments, she was able to say in a calmer voice. "Mother, I will not be a concert pianist. I see a concert pianist as being a show off, and I don't want to be a show off."

Brenda's mother sank into the nearest chair and just sat there shaking her head.

"This has been your dream," Brenda continued, facing her. "Since you could not succeed in your desire, you've tried to fulfill your dream through me. That's not fair. I should be able to have my own dream to fulfill." She took a deep breath, and said in a softer voice. "I love you, Mother, and I'm thankful for all you've done for me, but I want to fulfill my own dreams, not yours. Please let me make my own decisions about my future. I want to have time to study more to earn good grades so I can go to college. I want time for friends. Up till now I've had no friends until Annalisa came along and told me she saw a nice girl deep inside of me struggling to rise to the surface. She believes in me. She encourages me, and we think alike." Brenda wiped her eyes.

Mrs. Polanski stared at Brenda for several seconds, took a deep breath, then asked,

"What do you mean—you think alike?"

"Well, we both want to earn good grades in school, we both have goals of trying to find a career where we help other people. We both have high standards."

Brenda wasn't sure if her mother even heard her pleading. She just sat on the couch where she had collapsed, looking hurt.

"Speaking of high standards, Mother, I have never lied to you before—except for two weeks ago today. I went to the youth group meeting that Wednesday for the first time, when they were having a Thanksgiving Party. I know you thought I was home all evening practicing, and I'm sorry I deceived you. But I just felt like I'd die if I couldn't start having some fun. In fact, a few weeks earlier, I was seriously considering committing suicide. I probably would have, if I could have found enough sleeping pills."

Brenda's mother didn't answer. She just sat there like she was in shock.

Finally, Brenda went to her room to finish her homework and go to bed, where she tossed and turned most of the night.

The next morning, her mother acted terse and cold. Brenda tried to act polite before she went to school, but her mother wouldn't speak to her. That evening, her mother worked the evening shift again, so wasn't home till nearly midnight.

Friday morning Mrs. Hoffman called Brenda out of class to talk with her. She had a satisfied look on her face. "Remember, I told you the principal and I would try to talk with your mother? We saw her yesterday and I wanted to tell you the results. We convinced her to lighten up on her expectations of your practicing. We told her you need more time to study, and also more time to be a normal teenager. It took a bit of talking, but finally she agreed to let you set your own practice schedule and study schedule and that she would include you in any decisions about performances. She also agreed to let you go to youth group regularly with Annalisa."

"Wow! How did you do that?" Brenda asked.

Mrs. Hoffman smiled a sly smile. "We had another person present at this discussion. It was a parent-child counselor from the child abuse authorities. He made some good points.

Brenda felt like she was walking on air on her way back to class. Was it possible? Could she really begin to make some of her own decisions? She felt like running and leaping and...

But there was something she needed to do first. During lunch hour, Brenda discussed it with Annalisa, Todd, and Travis. "Do you think I should apologize?"

"What do you believe you did wrong?" Travis asked.

"I'm sure my mother believes I was wrong to say I won't be a concert pianist."

"What do you believe?" asked Todd.

"I believe it should be my own choice, and the counselor seems to agree with me."

"Then why would it be wrong to tell that to your mother?...as long as you did it in a kind way?" said Travis.

"Well, maybe it wasn't so kind to shout."

"Maybe," said Annalisa, "if you just ask her to forgive you for shouting at her, she will be willing to accept that you want to make some of your own decisions."

"Yes, you're right. I wasn't acting very respectful. I've resented her."

Brenda decided to go visit Mrs. Hoffman again during study hall. The counselor encouraged her to do what she could to reopen communication with her mother, but that she was old enough to make her own decisions about her future. When she went home after school, her mother was there.

"Mother, I thought you had to work this evening. What happened?"

"Nothing. I just told them I didn't feel well, so they gave me a sick day."

"What's the matter, Mother?" Brenda went over to her and sat down beside her."

"Oh, it's nothing physical. I'm just so upset."

"Mother, I am sorry for yelling at you. That wasn't respectful. Will you forgive me?"

"Oh, I don't blame you for yelling at me, after I yelled at you. I've been thinking all night and day about what you said. You didn't say anything wrong. You were just being honest about how you felt. It's just that I didn't like how you felt, but I suppose you can't help that." She picked at the pattern on her skirt.

"Brenda, I have to tell you I'm sorry for trying to push my dream onto you." Her voice sounded funny, like she was having difficulty pushing a large needle through a thick quilt. Brenda knew it was difficult for her to say this. "You are correct. Since I failed as a concert pianist, I wanted you to fulfill my dream. You are also correct in that you should have the right to choose your own dream to follow. Try to be patient with me, though, for I will be grieving the death of a dream for awhile."

"Thank you Mom. I know you wanted the best for me and I'm grateful to you for that. I'll make you proud of me in the future."

"I'm already proud of you, my daughter." Brenda and her mother hugged each other, then Brenda went to her room to finish homework while her mother sat in a chair and read a book.

Brenda's attitude was better than usual that Saturday when she went along with her mother's planned trip to the mall, where she was to play piano in the central square for an hour. She smiled at her mother, trying to help her feel better, and ended up actually enjoying doing the concert. Then they had ice cream in the Sweet Shoppe. Mother put her hand over Brenda's and looked her in the eyes. "Thank you for keeping this commitment and not embarrassing me. I appreciate that." Brenda noticed tears in her eyes.

"You're welcome," Brenda said, as her eyes misted up. "I don't want you to think I don't like to play piano at all. It's not that—it's just that I want to be part of making the decisions about what I do and I don't want to be forced to fit into a mold I can't fit into."

"That makes sense. Please forgive me."

"Yes, I do." Brenda replied. It seemed like they finally connected. She felt more joy and love toward her mother than she had for a long time.

That evening after supper, Brenda's smart phone rang. "Hello?" They talked awhile and then Brenda said, "Yes, I'd like to, but let me talk it over with Mother and call you back. Thanks Annalisa."

Brenda approached her mother fearfully. Maybe this would be going too far. She found her mother half asleep on the couch in front of the TV. "Mother, could I ask a big favor of you?"

Mother sat up straight and rubbed her eyes. "What is it, Brenda?"

"Annalisa has asked if I could stay overnight with her the day school lets out for Christmas vacation. That would be the 17th and I don't see anything else on the calendar, except that you are working evening shifts. She said I could either stay one night or for the whole weekend."

"What would you be doing? It wouldn't be any wild party, would it?"

"Oh no! Of course not. Annalisa doesn't go for wild parties. It would be just her and me, and her aunt would be there. She said we would just visit and watch movies or play table games. I really like Annalisa, and would like to become better friends with her."

Mother got up and looked at her planner. Brenda could see her mouth working, as if she was fighting with her emotions. "I suppose that would be all right. But before I say for sure, I'd like to talk with her aunt."

"That's fine." Brenda wrote on a piece of paper. "Here's her number. Her name is Miss Catherine Schuiteman."

Brenda was elated when her mother said later she could visit Annalisa for the weekend in two weeks. She called Annalisa back to tell her.

"Mother said I can stay either overnight and all day Saturday, or the whole weekend."

"That's great!" Annalisa replied. "If you stay the weekend, you can go to church with us."

Brenda wasn't sure what to say about that. "I'll let you know Monday which I decide."

30

The Roman Road

At lunchtime Monday, Brenda asked Annalisa if they could sit alone so they could talk privately. They found a quiet place in a corner.

Annalisa could see that Brenda was doing some serious thinking.

"May I ask what is on your mind Brenda?"

"Sure. When you first asked me to attend your youth group meeting at your church, I was not sure if I wanted to go with you to a church meeting. My Mother and I went to church when I was in elementary school, and she insisted I play the piano for the singing. She used to tell people that someday I would be a concert pianist. After we moved here, she was hired for the job she has now and she started to work on Sundays, so quit going to church. I stopped going to church, too, at that time, because I was tired of them expecting me to play piano all the time. Now I still feel uncomfortable with the idea of going to church."

Annalisa thought Brenda looked tense. "That's understandable," Annalisa said. "It's the fear of the unknown. But there would be no expectations of you at my church. You could just observe and listen, and if you don't want to go again, it's okay. If you decide not to go at all, that's okay, too. By the way, what would you like for dinner that Friday evening?"

"Surprise me with the dinner. I eat anything."

"My Aunt is a wonderful cook. She makes good, wholesome food that not only tastes good but keeps me healthy and well. So you're not allergic to anything?"

Brenda shook her head and smiled at Annalisa. "I think we're going to be good friends. Thank you."

"You're welcome. I'm anxious for these two weeks to go by quickly so we can enjoy our time together. We do have a piano, and would love to listen to you practice, if you wish."

The next two days passed quickly with Brenda and Annalisa eating lunch together with Todd and Travis or Mary Lou. They talked about classes and their busyness, or an upcoming aptitude test they had both signed up to take.

Wednesday, they went to youth group.

Annalisa and Brenda bounced out of the car at the church, amidst snow flurries. "Thanks for the ride, Aunt Catherine. See you after youth group."

They ran into the church just as Terry began. "Welcome to youth group tonight. Since this is the last youth group meeting before the New Year, we will do our annual presentation of the Roman Road. We want to tell you about God's plan of salvation. So sit by a friend and let's travel on the Roman road. Please turn to the book of Romans."

"Where is Romans?" whispered Brenda to Annalisa.

"It is in the New Testament after the four Gospels and Acts."

"Now," Terry said, "find Romans chapter 3, verse 23. The wording may be a little different, because I'm using the English Revised Version (ERV). It reads, 'All have sinned and are not good enough to share God's divine greatness," (Romans 3:23, ERV).' Terry looked around at the teenagers. "Do you understand that everyone is a sinner and, because of that, we cannot make our own way to God because he is perfect and sinless?"

Several people said, "Yes, we understand."

"The second verse is Romans 6:23. It says, "When people sin they earn what sin pays – death." (Romans 6:23, ERV).

"What does that mean?" asked a new girl.

Terry looked around the room. "Who can tell her what it means?"

Mary Ann raised her hand. "It means if you die without Jesus' forgiveness, you'll spend eternity separated from God. I don't want that to happen. I want to go to heaven when I die."

"I do too," said Mary Lou.

Carrie took a turn leading. "The third verse on the Roman Road is Romans 5:8. It tells us, 'But Christ died for us while we were still sinners.' (Romans 5:8 ERV)."

"Do you mean to tell me Jesus did that even though people were sinners and did not yet believe in Him?" asked Ralph.

"That's correct, Ralph," Carrie assured him. "That's God's love for everyone. He didn't have to do what he did;

he did it because he loves everyone and does not want anyone to die and spend eternity separated from Him."

"Well said," said Terry. "The next verse is Romans 10:13. "Yes, everyone who trusts in the Lord will be saved." (Romans 10:13 ERV)."

"Even me?" asked Brenda. "I've not been kind to people. I've been angry and spiteful." Her face began to turn pink. "The only person who has ever said they wanted to be my friend is Annalisa, and I don't know why she did."

"Brenda, I'm glad to be your friend and I know God loves you," said Annalisa.

"Brenda, I don't know much about you, but I know Annalisa is correct," said Terry. "God wants to forgive you and anyone else who asks him."

Terry turned a few pages in his Bible. "Have you all read the crucifixion story in the Bible? One version is found in Luke 23, and Luke 24 tells of the resurrection."

His wife, Carrie, chimed in again, "There's one last verse on the Roman Road," Carrie said. "This verse is for anyone who has accepted Jesus as their Savior. It says, 'So now, anyone who is in Christ Jesus is not judged guilty. (Romans 8:1 ERV).' Who can tell what this means?

"That means once you confess your sins and accept Jesus as your Savior, God forgives all your sins and chooses not to remember them," said Annalisa. "When you die, you enter into heaven as a forgiven sinner."

"Really?" Brenda said, "That is a comforting thought. All that anger I've held toward others will be forgiven and forgotten by God. I'll have to think about that."

"If you have any questions, come and see me. If there is anything I cannot answer I'll refer you to the pastor," said Terry. "Are there any other comments or questions?"

Many of the young people seemed to be deep in thought.

"Well kids, the time is growing late. It is time for you to go to your homes. Let us pray before you leave."

"Father in heaven, I thank you for this fine group of teenagers. I pray you will bless them and strengthen them for your service. Comfort them and wrap your loving arms around them and give them wisdom for their school work and peace in their hearts. In Jesus name, Amen."

Terry looked at Todd and Travis and asked them, "Would you stay a few minutes? I want to talk with you about something."

Brenda and Annalisa waited in the hall together for Todd and Travis to give them a ride. At first both girls were quiet. Then, Brenda asked Annalisa, "Are you a Christian?"

Annalisa replied, "Yes, I am."

"Why?" asked Brenda.

"Because I believe Jesus is the Christ, the Son of the Living God. He is my Savior and my Master. After my parents died, I asked God, *Why did my parents die? I asked you to keep them safe and return them home to me.* I was confused. I thought God had made a big mistake, but then I realized God does not make mistakes. He can see the end from the beginning. I had to trust God had a reason for what he had allowed to happen and someday I would learn that reason. That time may come before or after I die. I just trust that God loves me and will continue to take care of me. He provides for all my needs, including friendships.

I'm thankful for my several friends: Todd and Travis, the other members of the youth group here, and especially you, Brenda. I expect a long friendship with you."

"Thank you, Annalisa; I want a long friendship with you as well."

Just then, Todd and Travis walked up to them. "Ready?" Travis asked.

Todd opened the door of the covered yellow Jeep. "Allow me to help you into my chariot." Taking Annalisa's hand he held it gently as she stepped into his jeep. Then he walked around and did the same with Brenda. Both Brenda and Annalisa giggled.

"This chariot doesn't look like those in movies," commented Annalisa.

"Young lady, that is because this is an improved model of the ancient chariot. Notice the seats are cushioned, the windows open and close, there is space behind the seats for backpacks and food. The best part is, there are no horses to clean up after and care for," Todd said.

After driving a few blocks, he 'helped' Brenda out. Bowing low with a flourish, he said,"Good night, Lady Brenda. it was nice to see you."

"Good night, Sir Todd," giggled Brenda.

Annalisa jumped out and gave her a hug.

"I'll see you tomorrow," Brenda said. "Let's go to the library again after school."

"Yes, let's. Good night my friend," said Annalisa.

31

Aptitude Test

Friday Dec. 10th, Brenda and Annalisa went to the counselor's office and together they listened as Mrs. Hoffman instructed them about the test. "Be honest about the answers. Don't answer questions the way you think is expected, but rather the way you feel in your heart.

Make your choices clear. If you erase an answer to select another, erase as cleanly as possible. Return the test to me and I should have the results by Monday."

The following Monday, they made separate appointments to talk with Mrs. Hoffman to talk about their aptitude tests. She asked Brenda to tell about her feelings about music. "The aptitude test is inconclusive on this," she said. "Do you really dislike music?"

"No," Brenda said. "What I really dislike is my mother's obsession with the concert pianist career idea. "

Mrs. Hoffman waited, sensing she wanted to say more.

Brenda shifted uneasily in her chair, then answered in a quieter voice. "There's another reason I resent my mother's insistence upon this. My mother and dad often argued about many things, especially my music lessons. I liked my music lessons at first, but mother made me practice so long and more as I grew older. Dad said Mother was driving me too hard. "Let her be a little girl for a change," he would say. Mother would reply, "No! She is going to be a concert pianist and that takes constant effort." Finally, while I was in sixth grade, Mother told me I had a new teacher---a very expensive, advanced teacher. Dad hit the roof when he found out Mother had already paid for a year in advance on their credit card. Not long after that, he told Mother he thought they ought to get a divorce. Mother … didn't even seem to care."

Brenda began to choke up, and seemed unable to go on. But finally she blurted out, "We moved up here shortly after that, and my Dad committed suicide a month later." Then she let the sobs and the tears come. "I've resented her so much for that!"

"Oh, you poor Dear!" Mrs. Hoffman moved over next to her and hugged her. After several minutes she asked, "Do you want to know what I think?"

Brenda lifted her tear-filled eyes. "Yes, I do."

"I think your mother really needs counseling. But it won't improve the situation for you to remain resentful toward her. If you can forgive her, you will feel happier. I also think you don't have to fulfill your mother's dream. You need to be respectful, but tell her how you feel and proceed to fulfill your own dreams."

Brenda nodded, wiping her eyes again. "So I need to identify my dream and pursue it."

"Yes. According to your test results, Brenda, you have an exceptional aptitude for music, but also for something in the medical field or teaching. There are many options for vocations."

"I have thought of maybe going into nursing, or teaching."

"Those are good choices. You could teach music in elementary or high school, could combine teaching with music, or you could become minister of music in a church. If you choose a different career, you could volunteer in your spare time in various music positions. As I said, Brenda, there are many options. You don't need to plan out your whole life now. But I do think it is good to work toward a goal, even though you may change your mind later."

"What do you advise? I'm not sure my grades are good enough to get into college."

"Brenda, you are only a sophomore. You have time to bring your grades up. Your grade point average is 3 point, which isn't bad. If you can do well the rest of High School, you will have no trouble getting into college. Spend your time in high school taking what we call the college prep courses. If you wish, sign up for choir and band. Do you play other instruments?"

"Yes, in the elementary band, I played both clarinet and flute."

"You could also elect orchestra. This plan would keep you quite busy, but it would also help prepare you for college. And it might help you earn some good music scholarships. Pianists are usually in demand at colleges."

"Do you have to major in music if you get a music scholarship?"

"No, you don't. You could still pursue your dream to be a doctor. It's the college grades that matter the most for getting accepted into medical school. Your SAT score shows you have the ability, and this test shows you do have a definite aptitude for that."

"Thank you, Mrs. Hoffman. Now I have a direction to go and a goal to try to achieve."

"You sound like an intelligent girl. I wish you well, and I am here whenever you have questions and especially when you begin to think about college and scholarships. Continue to earn good grades and you could win many scholarships which would reduce college costs."

"Thank you again," said Brenda.

When she left the office, Brenda took her permit slip back to her study hall teacher just as the bell rang. She found Annalisa waiting in the hall.

"Did you find answers to your questions?"

Brenda smiled. "Yes, I did. I now have a direction to follow. My goal for now is to bring my grades up and go to a liberal arts college after graduation. I'm sure Mother will not be pleased with my choices, but it's my life, not hers. I must follow my goals." They began walking home. "Please, Annalisa, will you pray for me and ask God to help me in my relationship with my mother?"

"Of course I will." She took Brenda's hand and spoke a short prayer.

"What did Mrs. Hoffman say about your test?"

"As we expected, she said I have great aptitude for being a teacher. But one thing surprised me. She suggested I go into social work."

"That doesn't surprise me, Annalisa. You've done a great job counseling me." They both laughed, then Annalisa walked Brenda home. "See you later."

Dinner the next Friday night consisted of breaded pork chops, mashed potatoes and gravy, mixed vegetables, rolls, with milk or water. "Aunt Catherine, you certainly are the good cook that Annalisa boasted you to be. Dinner was delicious. What is your secret?"

"There's no secret." Aunt Catherine smiled. "Take a home economics cooking class in school, use a good cookbook, and practice a lot. If you enjoy cooking and the people you cook for enjoy and compliment you on your cooking, that helps, too. You are welcome to visit and enjoy a meal anytime you wish. Now I would appreciate some help with the dishes."

"I knew you'd say that, you're always looking for dishwashers," moaned Annalisa.

"Oh, you poor girl, are you afraid you'll get dish pan hands?" teased Aunt Catherine.

"Of course," said Annalisa, "hot water dries the skin and I'll look old before my time."

"Well then, it's a good thing we have an automatic dishwasher. But there are a few things that won't fit or need to be washed by hand.

"I'll wash and you dry," said Brenda.

After the kitchen was cleaned up, Annalisa announced "We're going upstairs to my room for 'girl talk.'"

Aunt Catherine smiled. "All right. Have a fun time. I'll be up later with a bedtime snack for both of you." said Aunt Catherine.

"That sounds good," said Brenda, "I'm always hungry, as you can tell by my size."

"Brenda, I think you are just about the right size, and you are a pretty girl."

"Thank you, Aunt Catherine, you are kind." The two girls went upstairs.

"Let's watch a movie. Do you want something deep and involved, or something light?"

"Let's choose something light," Brenda replied.

Annalisa held out some Veggie Tales. "I know they're for kids, but I get a kick out of them." She let Brenda choose which one. As they watched, they munched on popcorn and sipped on flavored water. They laughed at the Silly Songs of Larry and Bob, then watched the story.

The movie was a story about prayer. When it was finished, Annalisa said, "Brenda, do you pray?"

"I haven't prayed since I was twelve, because it didn't seem like God heard me."

"You mean about your Mom and Dad?"

"Yes."

"I know the feeling. I had prayed that God would bring my parents safely back to me."

Both girls sat quietly for a couple minutes, thinking. Annalisa felt she and Brenda could understand each other's feelings better than most people. She reflected on what she believed. "I know God hears our prayers. But God knows better than we do what is best for everyone in the whole scheme of things. To give a simple example, one person may pray for rain because they have dry crops, while another is praying for sunshine because they want to have a picnic.

God has to decide what is best for everyone. Sometimes he says 'No' to his beloved children. I believe what Mrs. Hoffman said, 'God is holy and righteous,' therefore I can trust him to do what's best for me as long as I'm fitting into his plans for me."

Brenda huffed. "So you think it must be ' best' for you that your parents died?

"God must have some reason to allow it to happen. All I know is that God is good and he loves me. He loved my parents, and they are with him in joy and happiness now."

Brenda's voice rose, her face contorted. "How can a good, loving God stand still for all this evil? It's wrong that people get divorced, that they commit suicide, that parents are killed in airplane crashes." She got up to pace as her words took on intensity. "It's wrong that toddlers are killed by abusive parents, that college students are murdered in the park, that Jews were gassed in the holocaust. If God is good, why doesn't he do something about all that?" Brenda was crying by now. There was deep pain in her eyes as she looked to Annalisa for answers.

Annalisa went to her friend and hugged her. At first Brenda was stiff, but then she loosened up and let herself cry from the bottom of her heart while Annalisa held her. When she finally calmed down and wiped her face and blew her nose, Annalisa said, "You're right. Of course it is wrong. Evil is rampant in this world because the devil is at work."

Annalisa led Brenda to the padded window seat and they both sat down. She continued,

"But God does not 'stand still' for it as you say. He provided a solution. God himself, in the form of Jesus Christ, paid the price for humanity's sin of obeying the devil instead of obeying God. No matter how 'good' we are, we have all disobeyed God. Yet, if we believe in Jesus Christ and what he did for us, we repent and submit to God. Then he is able to work in our lives for 'good' by transforming our lives."

Brenda looked at Annalisa. "I'd like to believe that. I wish..." She stopped.

"Brenda, if you pray sincerely, God will hear your prayer. He loves you deeply and wants a loving relationship with you, too. I think God is seeking you and if you turn to him, he will hear your prayer and answer you."

"Do you really think so? I've been so angry and said and done things I'm not proud of."

"God loves you, I know. If you confess your sins and ask for his help, he'll welcome you with open arms."

Brenda sat quietly, looking at her hands.

Annalisa didn't want to push too hard. *Guide me, Holy Spirit.*

When Brenda looked up at her, she quietly suggested,

"Why don't you pray now? Just tell him all that is on your mind."

"All right, I will." She shifted on the window seat, then folded her hands and closed her eyes. "God, it's been a long time since I prayed to you, and I'm not sure I ever really knew how. But I want to learn how. I want to learn to trust you. Amen."

Annalisa waited, sensing Brenda wanted to confide in her further.

Brenda cleared her throat. "I prayed a lot for them that summer. It didn't seem to do any good. But there was one more thing I prayed for after we moved to Gardenia."

"Would you mind telling me about that?" Annalisa repositioned herself on the pillows.

Brenda looked a little hesitant. Then she forged ahead. "I felt so worthless, like my mother couldn't love me unless I fulfilled her dream, and my dad couldn't stand to be around me because I was with her. Yet, he didn't ask me to go with him. I wanted to do something great to earn their love, to be worth something in their eyes. So I entered a contest to write a fiction story. I enjoyed writing and imagining things, and I really thought I could win. The story would be printed in the newspaper and my parents would see it and realize how special I was. They would set aside their selfishness and indifference to me, forget all about the concert pianist obsession and encourage me to be a writer, in a happy home with two loving parents."

Annalisa listened intently. "You didn't win the contest?" She could see the pain in Brenda's eyes and wished she could take it away.

"I didn't win the contest. My dad committed suicide a week later. My mother continued her obsession and acted like she hardly knew who I really am."

"Oh, Brenda, I'm so sorry! You wanted it so badly."

Brenda hesitated, then plunged ahead to tell the rest. "You asked me once why I was so mean to you ever since you met me in seventh grade. This is the reason, although

I'm not holding it against you any longer. You won that contest."

Annalisa felt her blood drain out of her face. *I'd forgotten all about that contest! What did I even write about?* She burst into tears as the sense sank in of how Brenda must have felt. "Brenda, I'm so sorry! I wish..."

Brenda took her hand. She said in a quiet voice, "I realized later my hopes had been unrealistic, but I was just so jealous of you. You seemed to live a charmed life. You were pretty, popular, smart, a good writer. I couldn't do anything as well as you. I'm sorry now for jealousy and for being so mean to you. Will you please forgive me?" She looked sincerely at Annalisa.

Annalisa could only nod, she was still crying so hard. Now she understood that Brenda's actions had been a cry from a broken heart. But now, God was beginning to mend that heart. The two girls talked and prayed and talked some more until they both felt something lift from their hearts. Brenda thought it felt like shackles were removed. Annalisa felt like Jesus had lifted off her heart the burden he had earlier laid there for her to bear.

32

A Change in Brenda

The next morning, Brenda and Annalisa awoke late to a sunny day inside and out. When they came down stairs, Aunt Catherine had just finished preparing a brunch of scrambled eggs, sausage, and fruit along with toast.

"Aunt Catherine, thank you so much. That was good. I'm not hungry anymore now," said Brenda. After breakfast they went for a long walk, enjoying the 50-degree temperature.

After lunch, Brenda ran her fingers up the piano. "May I play your piano?" She asked.

"I didn't know you played," said Aunt Catherine. "Of course you may."

Brenda sat at the piano and played several happy tunes, some hymns, and a few popular tunes. When she stopped playing and turned around Aunt Catherine sat on the sofa gazing at her. She said, "Brenda, that was beautiful. You have a lot of talent. You certainly are a skilled pianist."

"Thank you." She told Catherine about the recent change in her household, after the counselor had spoken with her mother. "I feel freer now to play for enjoyment," she said.

By this time, it was the middle of the afternoon. Brenda stood up and looked at Annalisa and Catherine. "My mother must be leaving for work about now. I feel I should go home and do the Saturday cleaning. Mother has had a big shock, and I want to try to ease the burden a little."

"That is thoughtful, Brenda. We have enjoyed having you and hope you come again."

As the girls walked to Brenda's home, Brenda thanked Annalisa for the good time and said she'd like to attend the next youth group meeting.

"Good," said Annalisa. "We'll pick you up at 6:30. That's the Christmas party night."

Sunday morning, Brenda rose early and began sorting through her outfits. *What shall I wear today? I want to surprise Annalisa by going to church, and sit by her if I can find room. I should wear something that is subdued and conservative, not something that shouts, like the color red. Ah, here's my brown dress. Plain, no frills, not too short, not too long, high collar and short sleeves.* Gathering her clothing Brenda walked to the bathroom only to find her mother already there doing her hair before going to work.

"Good morning Brenda. I see by the clothes on your arm that you are planning to go somewhere."

"Yes, mother, I thought I would go to church this morning. If I arrive early enough maybe I can sit by Annalisa and she can help me understand the service."

"Good thought. I hope you have a good time."

"I wish you could go with me."

Brenda's mother looked at her with a questioning look. "I know you have resented me. I didn't think you'd want to be seen with me."

"Forgive me for resenting you, Mother. It's just that I felt almost like a slave who had to do what his owner said. I didn't like that feeling. I wanted to be free to make my own choices."

"I never thought of it that way. I thought I was doing what was best."

"I know you want what is best for me because you love me. I love you, too, and am grateful for all you've done for me."

Dressing quickly Brenda left the house and quickly walked to church. When she arrived, she followed other people inside and stood searching for Annalisa. Soon she found her and saw an empty seat next to her. Walking down the aisle she asked Annalisa if she could sit next to her.

"Of course you may," said Annalisa, with a smile. "I'm so glad you are here." Annalisa asked in a whisper, "What made you decide to come today?"

"You." Brenda smiled at Annalisa. "You are so different from a lot of the other kids at school. I want what you have. You are a special person, so kind and helpful. If I lost my mother like you lost your parents, I would be angry at everyone. I wouldn't be fit to live with and nobody would want to be my friend like you are doing. Please tell me your secret."

"Sure, Brenda. My secret is my relationship with Jesus Christ. I study the Bible and try to be just like Jesus."

"What do you mean, be like Jesus?"

"Jesus never sinned. He was kind and compassionate. He loved everyone, even those who killed Him. He forgave them for their anger and hatred."

"That must have been very difficult," said Brenda.

"Yes, I'm sure it was, but love helps you to be kind and compassionate in spite of how others treat you." Both girls stopped talking as the Prelude began.

The congregation sang and prayed, and Pastor Brady got up to speak. "My sermon text is John 3:16, probably the best known text in the Bible. Turn in your Bible to that text, and let's read it together."

Annalisa quietly opened her Bible to the text page and pointed it out to Brenda, whose eyes opened wide as she read it silently. As the Pastor spoke, Brenda thought he was speaking directly to her.

"God loves you and wants the best for you. He will stay by you, help you with your problems, and stand between you and Satan to protect you from Satan's lies. Why does he do that? Because he loves you. His love is different than selfish human love; it is pure love that seeks only what is best for a person. The Greeks call it agape love. It is a love that is unselfish and unconditional for another person."

When he finished his sermon, the congregation sang another hymn and the doxology. Annalisa and Brenda quietly went to the educational wing of the church and found a room with no one inside.

"Brenda, I'm happy you came to church today. You look nice in that brown dress."

"Thank you, Annalisa, you look nice too. Now, I've decided I want to be a Christian, as you are. What do I do or say? I don't know how to become a Christian," commented Brenda.

"It's easy. Do you believe that Jesus is God's Son and he came to this earth for the express purpose of giving his life to pay for our sins?" Annalisa asked.

"Yes, I believe he is the only way to be saved."

"Then, Brenda, just pray to God, confess that you are a sinner, ask God to forgive you for your sins, and live in your life."

"But do I need to name all my sins? That would take years of time."

"No, you just need to tell God you are a sinner and ask Him to forgive your sins. He already knows about all of your sins."

"Okay, stop me if I'm wrong. Dear Father in heaven, I confess to you that I have sinned. Please forgive me and I accept Jesus' death on the cross as the only payment for my sins. Please come and live in my life, I give myself to you. In Jesus name I pray this prayer, Amen."

Brenda felt a peace come into her life that she had never known. She opened her eyes and saw Annalisa with tears in her eyes. "Why are you crying, Annalisa?"

"Brenda, these are tears of joy. Now you can look forward to spending eternity in heaven with God, and you are now my sister in Christ. I've always wanted a sister, and now you are it. I'm so happy."

Just then the door to the room opened and Annalisa's Aunt Catherine and Pastor Brady walked into the room. "So here you are," said Annalisa's aunt. I've been looking for you."

"I have big news for you. I want to introduce you to the newest member of God's family. Tell them, Brenda."

"Annalisa just helped me ask Jesus to be my Savior."

"Brenda, I'm so glad. The Bible says there's joy in heaven over a sinner who repents. I can almost hear the angel choir singing and bells ringing." Aunt Catherine threw her arms around Brenda and hugged her close. Pastor Brady congratulated Brenda and shook her hand. "This girl needs a tissue; someone give her one. If you'll follow me, Brenda, I have something to give to you."

"What might that be?" Brenda asked, wiping her eyes.

"We usually give a Bible to every new believer, but I understand Annalisa has already given you one, so here is a book called *Jesus Calling*. All we ask is that you develop the habit of reading it every day and consider becoming a part of our church."

All Brenda could say was, "Thank you."

Aunt Catherine said, "If you have no plans for dinner today, you are welcome to our home." She accepted the invitation and they had a wonderful couple hours.

That evening, when Brenda's mother came home from work, Brenda had already set the table and opened cans of chunky soup for supper. "Mother, I know things are difficult for you, trying to support me and provide for me. I'll try to help out more here at home and be a more responsible girl. I'm thinking of taking a cooking class next fall. Maybe I can start some of our meals before you come home from work. I'll even help with drying the dishes."

Brenda's mother stood with her mouth open, speechless.

"Mom, you're not having a heart attack are you?" asked Brenda.

Suddenly her Mom burst into a smile. "Brenda, I would really appreciate the help in the kitchen. Your help would make life easier for me." With that said she threw her arms around Brenda and hugged her tightly.

"Mom, please don't squeeze me so hard, I'm not a toothpaste tube," Brenda laughed.

Her mother laughed, also, and let go. "What has happened to change your attitude?"

"I have become a Christian, Mother. After church this morning, Annalisa helped me to pray and ask Jesus Christ to be my Savior. After I prayed, I felt a great sense of peace and love.

Epilogue

nnalisa had great fun the night of the youth group party. She felt glad that Brenda seemed to be having a wonderful time, also. Annalisa thought of the heaviness and heartache she'd felt after receiving the news of her parents' deaths and couldn't help comparing. Her heart felt so much lighter now than it had for the past three months.

Thank you, Lord, for getting me through that terrible time. I felt like some unseen force was pulling me down into the dredges. Everything seemed so senseless, like why should the world go on functioning when my beloved parents were dead? But now I feel like they've simply gone on a trip and I'll see them again someday. I miss them, Lord, but I thank you for being with me always, and I thank you for my aunt and my friends. Most of all, thank you for giving me a purpose in befriending Brenda. Please enable me to succeed in helping her in whatever further way you wish. Her acceptance of you has given me a new lease on life.

At the Party, Annalisa told the youth group members that Brenda had accepted Jesus as her Savior the past Sunday morning. All the girls crowded around Brenda and hugged her. The boys didn't hug Brenda, but they cheered.

"This calls for a celebration," said Bill. Immediately he began to sing Amazing Grace.

He hadn't sung more than three measures when loud moans and groans were heard from the group. "What's wrong," asked Bill. "This group doesn't like the song I chose?"

"It's not the song," laughed everyone. "You just can't carry a tune," said Annalisa.

"Maybe I can help," said Brenda as she went to the piano.

Annalisa stepped back and covered her mouth with her hands. Soon a beautiful rendition of Amazing Grace filled the room. Brenda played through one verse before she stopped. "Don't you like my playing?"

"We love your playing," said everyone, "we just didn't know you could play so well."

Brenda started playing again. "Are you going to sing or should I sit back down?"

"Play, play, please play and we will all sing along." When one song finished someone set a book with a song in front of her and called out another title. Others followed likewise. After several songs, it was time for the entire youth group to go home.

"Brenda, we hope you come every week. Your piano playing was extra special," said Bill. "You made us sound good."

"Thank you," said Brenda with a grin. "You sounded great to me."